6-17-09

To Ar[...]

Thank you for getting the "Point" It so nice to hear from good friends of Mom & Dad.

Greg Sullivan

# Pike Point
## And the Good Lord's Earth

Greg Suhonen

authorHOUSE®

*AuthorHouse*™
*1663 Liberty Drive*
*Bloomington, IN 47403*
*www.authorhouse.com*
*Phone: 1-800-839-8640*

© *2009 Greg Suhonen. All rights reserved.*

*No part of this book may be reproduced, stored in a retrieval system, or transmitted by any means without the written permission of the author.*

*First published by AuthorHouse 4/13/2009*

*ISBN: 978-1-4389-7594-8 (e)*
*ISBN: 978-1-4389-7593-1 (sc)*
*ISBN: 978-1-4389-7595-5 (hc)*

*Library of Congress Control Number: 2009903336*

*Printed in the United States of America*
*Bloomington, Indiana*

*This book is printed on acid-free paper.*

And now,
these three remain:
faith, hope and love.
But the greatest of these is love.

St. Paul the Apostle

# May 1922

Normally, Paavo was a patient man. He was quiet and soft-spoken, almost to the point of being shy. Most people who first met him, if asked, would say he was polite and respectful. Even so, were he to be caught in a rare, unguarded moment, those around him would be treated to a good-natured glimpse of his razor-sharp wit. Paavo was an easy man to like.

But not this morning. This morning was different. Politeness and respect were the farthest things from Paavo's mind because right now he would like nothing better than to rip the huge map right off the wall and tear it into ten thousand satisfying shreds. A sly grin crept into one corner of his mouth when the image of him standing ankle-deep in the hopelessly torn up piece of paper entered his thoughts. Besides, all of his happy plans were in ruins, so really, he had nothing left to lose by having a frenzied fit.

Feeling as though he'd just been given the go-ahead, an irresistible temptation forced Paavo's hands from his pockets. Very casually, he scanned each end of the courthouse hallway. The few people he saw seemed too preoccupied with their own affairs to pay any notice of him. If he did actually this, he'd have to be quick. No standing around in a pile of scrap paper admiring his dirty work. One big pull, Paavo decided, then he would run. Then he would feel so much better.

Then he hesitated.

And in that split-second pause, the better part of Paavo's quiet nature took over. What in the world had come over him, he wondered. That type of behavior wasn't like him at all. This was foolishness. And think of how humiliating, to be the center of that kind of attention. He had better get a grip and he had better do it now, otherwise the last three years of his life would be for nothing.

Red-faced and scolded by his own thoughts, Paavo slid his hands back into his pockets. But the angry frustration stayed in his head and was reason enough for Paavo allowing himself to stab a nasty glare back at the smug map. That feeble act did little to rid him from the strong urge to yank the drawing down from the wall. So, as a poor substitute, Paavo pinched the brim of his day-old tweed cap and snatched it off the top of his head. He felt much better when the hat slapped sharply against his thigh. With his free hand, Paavo scratched around at his sandy blond hair. That much accomplished, he set the stiff cap back in place only to shift it around every few seconds. He could find no peaceful place for it. He soon gave up the search for a comfortable spot and simply pulled down hard on the brim, wedging the cap tightly to his head.

Paavo had been here for a good while, staring, studying, trying to make some sense of the strange-looking map but there were just too many lines, and too many numbers. They all seemed to run together into a jumbled, nonsensical mess.

Earlier, others had come to gaze upon the map. Business people, he had assumed, with their dark, pin-striped suits and looping watch fobs that made him feel inadequate and out of place. These important people never lingered very long, stopping for only a minute or two as they carefully jotted down the numbers and letters they had deciphered from the perplexing drawing. Everyone seemed to understand what they were doing. Everyone, that is, except him.

But no one had come to read the map for some time and now Paavo regretted he had not asked a few harmless questions. He justified his lack of nerve by telling himself those people probably wouldn't have been able to understand him anyway. Paavo's shy reserve had cost him though, because left on his own he'd had no success in coaxing any secrets from the stubborn map. The long half-hour he had been here was a total waste. To make matters worse, he was running out of time.

A quick glance up at the hard-ticking wall clock prompted Paavo to again slide the hat from his head. He willed his eyes back onto the map and unconsciously twisted the cap into a tight mass, as if wringing it free of any water.

The closely-packed elevation lines of the topographical map had Paavo baffled. He had never seen anything quite like it. Adding to his confusion, this region, this Minnesota Arrowhead, also contained thousands of streams, rivers and lakes. All these extra, random lines were represented on the plat and they snaked and scattered themselves freely across the entire length of the paper. The busy map was also littered with dozens of pins, and to each pin, a white paper flag had been attached. Each flag was lettered and numbered but that meant nothing to Paavo. He could not read English.

He hadn't anticipated anything like this, not the need to gather information from the map, or the necessity to understand the written word. Paavo felt as if he had recklessly jumped into fast-moving water that was way over his head. His hope of buying land was fading away with each passing second. He edged closer to the wall and leaned in, his blue eyes squeezed into a deep squint.

It did not help.

His attention shifted to a large, blank area on the right, a westerly slice of Lake Superior, and the only feature he could correctly identify.

"A little child know dat," he muttered quietly to himself.

Paavo shook his head and backed away from the wall. He looked left, then right, trying to spot someone, anyone, who could help. Too late, the hallway of the Duluth Courthouse was nearly deserted and no help came. Paavo looked up to the clock once more and immediately turned away, avoiding the blunt reality that the county land auction would be starting at any minute. Nevertheless, the undeniable truth of the matter managed to sink in and Paavo let out a tired sigh, releasing the troubled tension that had built up inside of him.

He had run out of time.

In English, Paavo whispered, "It be over."

He donned the distorted hat and jammed his hands deep into his pockets, ready to leave. He stopped short when the fingers of his left hand curled around a tight roll of hard-earned money.

In Finnish, Paavo thought, "Eight hundred dollars. Surely that would have been enough money to get the land I want."

He thought too, about the many hours of back-breaking work that had helped him earn his small fortune. For the past three years, each spring, summer and fall, he had bored, hammered and loaded iron-rich ore from the murky depths of a seasonal underground mine. In each winter of those three years, he had chopped, sawed and froze in the logging camps of northern Minnesota. He had scrimped and saved. He had worked to exhaustion and gone without, just to get to this very day, in this very place; all those countless hours of harsh labor he had endured; all for the chance to bid on some land. And now that he was finally here, he didn't even know where to begin. All he knew was this poorly-planned disaster was over.

"Nothing but a far-fetched dream," he decided sadly.

Paavo gave one final look to the unfeeling map, hoping for a last-second miracle. It offered nothing.

"Time to go," he whispered.

"Excuse me?"

The high pitched voice was unexpected and Paavo nearly jumped out of his new shoes. He spun to his right but saw no one there.

"May I help you?"

This time the voice also came with a tug at his opposite sleeve. He turned toward the tug and looked down to see a very short and very stout woman staring up at him.

"May I help you, young man?" she repeated.

Paavo nodded slightly and frowned, unsure of what the old lady could do for him.

"I've been watching you from my office for some time," she said, pointing to an open doorway directly behind them. "Are you here for the land auction?"

She talked very fast, as did most Americans. He had to pause so he could absorb the meaning of her words.

"Ya, I neet help wit lant aukshun," Paavo answered, forcing a small smile.

She smiled back, held out her hand and spoke slower, after hearing his heavy accent.

"Good morning. My name is Eva St.Jude. I work here at the courthouse…in the Land Department."

"Paavo Maki," he said, shaking her hand while automatically taking off his cap.

"Very good. Now, let us get started."

Eva lifted the eyeglasses that hung loosely from the light chain around her neck and perched them near the tip of her nose. She gave Paavo a serious, teacher-type look.

"Where are you from, Mr. Maki?"

"Finland," he said proudly.

"No. No. My mistake. I meant, where do you live *now*? I'm guessing, that you want to bid on land, close to where you live."

"I liff close by Ely."

"My, you certainly have come a long way, haven't you?"

Paavo nodded and stole another glance up at the clock. Less than a minute left. Eva turned to the map and magically pulled out a pencil from the backside of her braided hair-do. Careful not to disturb any of the pins on the map, she lightly touched the pencil to a large black dot on the western tip of Lake Superior.

"This is where we are, in Duluth, at the County Courthouse… Okay?"

She waited for his assent. He nodded quickly.

"Very good." Slowly, she ran the pencil tip up the map, stopping it at a smaller black dot. "And this, is the town of Ely."

"Ely!"

Paavo's face flushed with excitement. He had his bearings. His eyes scanned up, stopping a short distance north of the small speck. One of the dark outlines he stared at…Yes, there it was!

"Lust Vomen Lek!" he blurted out.

"What!?"

It was Eva's turn to be startled.

"Lust…Vomen…Lek." Paavo said it slower, his pronunciation sounding exactly the same.

"I'm afraid I don't understand, Mr. Maki."

Eva couldn't tell if he was speaking Finn or English. Paavo quickly tried a different approach.

"Pike Point…un Lust Vomen Lek."

Eva's eyes opened wide.

"Ahhh, now I get it. The parcel you want to bid on, is land that is located on *Lost Woman Lake*! Pike Point to be exact."

"Ya!...Yes!" Paavo could barely contain himself. "I come to pid munny un Pike Point."

He watched closely as Eva's pencil tracked north of Ely and stopped at the uppermost pin on the map. It was marked: "Lot No.1- Parcel 10161932"

Paavo had just recognized the shape of the lake as Lost Woman, with its' jagged shoreline and full myriad of its many islands. He watched as Eva rose to her tiptoes and pulled the tiny flag off the map, although his eyes remained on the small jut of land where the pin had been pulled out. The tiny Point looked so insignificant up there on the wall. But Paavo knew better. He had been out to look over the site three times, and each time, he considered it a wonder.

"If I could ever be so lucky," he always thought.

The base of Pike Point was nearly five-hundred feet wide and its peninsula aimed due north. The long neck of land narrowed, widened again in the middle, and finally finished into a hooked-shaped end. A quiet, circular bay hugged the west shore, with the open water of Lost Woman to the north and east. Scattered all along the nearly half-mile length of the Point were huge Norway and White Pine. Balsam Fir, Jack Pine and Upland Spruce also grew there. There was even a small smattering of White Birch. The natural acidity of the fallen pine needles had hindered any brushy, cluttering undergrowth allowing a clear view of the lake from almost anywhere Paavo stood. The tall, evergreen canopy furnished filtered light to the forest floor below and bestowed upon it a soft shade and a soothing presence.

It was perfect. The first time he set eyes on it he hoped out loud that a timber company would not want to bid on this remote, isolated parcel of land.

"They will clear cut and ruin it," he knew.

He'd seen that sort of thing happen before.

On each of his three trips to the Point, Paavo had wandered the entire loop of the rocky shoreline. He would stop every so often and look over the sparkling-blue water to the green, pine-packed islands that dotted Lost Woman Lake, mesmerized by the beauty of what his eyes were taking in.

"This is it," he would think. "The land I've been waiting for."

And after each visit, before leaving Pike Point, Paavo would stop and offer a meek but hopeful prayer, thinking all the while, perhaps he was asking for too much.

Eva's voice brought him back to the business at hand.

"Oh dear," she said, staring at the flagged pin she had just pulled out. "Pike Point is Lot Number One. That means it's the first parcel up for sale. You had better hurry upstairs, Mr. Maki. It's nine o'clock. The auction may have already started."

Her last sentence need not have been said. She turned toward her young student only to see Paavo sprinting up the nearby staircase.

"Ask for Room Three-Oh-Nine!" she shouted. "And good luck to you!"

Eva stretched up and placed the pin back on the map. She stared up at the noisy clock and made a mental note to have it replaced. The constant ticking was very annoying. Eva smirked when she looked again at the empty stairwell.

"That's right. Good luck, Paavo Maki. God knows you'll need it."

One hour later, a smiling clerk handed the Certificate of Title for Pike Point to a rattled Paavo. Before leaving, Paavo thanked the nice man again, only this time he said it in English.

The hectic proceedings of the auction, and the confusing paperwork that followed, had flown by so rapidly that all of it felt like a confusing blur. Paavo searched around in the growing bustle of the courthouse for a quiet place where he could be alone. Gradually making his way down to the first floor, Paavo found an empty restroom. He leaned lightly on the lavatory sink and dropped his new cap into the waste basket. Very carefully, as though the stiff paper may break apart before his eyes, he unfurled the deed. He stared at it for a long time, knowing that in his hands, he held his dreams. From this day forward his life would be much different - much better.

The seals, stamps and signatures meant little to Paavo, nor did he understand the printed words. What he did understand was this document represented a new beginning; not only for him, but for any that may follow in his footsteps. Pike Point was the perfect place to start over.

With that happy thought, Paavo's heart saddened when his mind flashed back to the dire circumstances that had caused him to leave Finland. In 1917, at the age of eighteen, he had buried both parents and a younger brother after an influenza outbreak swept through their small village. That same winter a fierce civil war broke out, with the Germans and Russians taking up opposite sides in the conflict, in a bitter struggle to gain political control of his country.

In the face of all that turmoil Paavo could think of no good reasons to stay any longer. It was time to leave. Hard though it was, Paavo sold the old family homestead and said a last goodbye to his departed family. He tucked his money into a shoe, lied about his age and left for America.

April of 1919 would find him at Ellis Island in New York, then on to Minnesota, where so many Finns had come before him. A very fine place, he had been told. A place where he could find plenty of work; and if you went up north, that place would remind him of Finland. Except, maybe it was a little colder.

And now, five years later, after losing everything, and thousands of miles from his homeland, here he was, the proud owner of some of the most beautiful land he had ever seen. Unlike the Old Country he'd left behind, anything was possible in this part of the world. All you had to do was work hard, try your best, and good things happened. Paavo agreed with the phrase his fellow immigrants had repeated to him, so many times.

"Only in America," he whispered.

Paavo nodded ruefully, reminding himself that only one short hour ago he had almost quit and run out on his dream.

"What if I had given up back in Finland, like I nearly did today?"

Paavo knew the answer even as he asked himself the question. There would be no America and no Pike Point. Life in the Old Country would have been dreary, and lonesome. A sad life. A life filled with only mindless work and too much hard bread.

"Never again will I be that weak," he vowed silently.

It was a priceless lesson Paavo would carry with him the rest his life.

From his very first visit to Pike Point, Paavo had envisioned a whole new way of life. The lake and surrounding land could feed and sustain him, year-round if need be. The Point could not only provide the materials for shelter, it also offered a solid place on which to build that new way of life.

Ahead of him lay much hard work, but after today, any hard work he did would benefit him, not someone else. Never again would he have to sweat and slog his way through that dripping, dark mine. No more would he numb and deaden his spirit in the biting, brutal conditions of a winter logging camp. His future was in his own hands. The prospect of being in charge of his own life left him feeling very good inside.

Paavo's final bid of seven hundred dollars had silenced his only bidding competitor, the Laurentian Lumber Company. After paying a fifty-cent filing fee, Paavo found himself with nearly one hundred dollars left in his pocket. More than enough money for him to get started.

"Oh! I must not forget to tank Miss Eva for her help to me," he said out loud. "No Pike Point wittout her."

As Paavo heard his words echo around the empty room, a whole new awareness awakened inside of him. Could it be that his chance encounter with the kindly Eva was actually a reply to the soft-spoken prayers he had made out on Pike Point?

The thought of such a miraculous possibility sent a heavy wave of chills up and down his spine. The longer the belief clung to him, the more Paavo realized that it had to be true - he had given up, so Eva was sent to help him. His prayers had been answered.

Then, without warning, the significance of what had taken place and intense emotions of the day overwhelmed his usual calm. Paavo tried, but he could not stop the tears that rolled down his face and landed on the treasured paper he held in his trembling hands.

Totally humbled and forever grateful for the gift he had been given, Paavo raised his head and directed his eyes beyond the ceiling above.

"Thank You," he said…over and over.

~

'Sisu' the Finns call it.

Americans have a hundred different names for it…courage, strength, determination…guts.

It was an important word that Paavo would repeat to himself a thousand times over the years.

"Sisu," he would whisper. "Your family needs you."

The remainder of his life, Paavo never let them down…ever.

# Pike Point

## May 1992

Ray Maki stood at the end of his dock looking out over the icy-blue water of Lost Woman Lake. In front of him lay a scene of peaceful, primeval beauty. The morning sun had yet to rise above the trees on the far off eastern shore and a soft blend of pinks and blues mingled in with the clouds, their shifting images mirrored on the surface of the lake. The blackened shadows of the far-off landscape and neighboring islands also reflected off the glassy water, in sharp contrast to the sky's morning colors.

All too soon, a light breeze arrived from somewhere and instantly smudged the lake's portrait, spoiling the perfect picture. But the wind made up for Ray's visual loss by carrying to him the sweet smell of the pines. All was quiet, save for the renewed flutter of waves lapping at the rocky shore. The absolute beauty and pureness of the setting convinced Ray, once again, there could be no other place like this on Earth.

As a young boy, Pike Point and Lost Woman Lake had been his back yard and his playground. He, his younger sister Kyla, and their friends had spent endless hours here, swimming, exploring, and totally enjoying their huge outdoor haven. This was a safe, wondrous spot for a small boy to grow up. Aside from the sudden loss of his father when he was thirteen, Ray had only fond memories of his early youth; thanks to the unwavering strength of his grandfather Paavo, and the tenderhearted love of his mother Ellie.

After Ray had grown into his mid-teens, his private playground expanded - considerably. Just beyond the front doorstep of his boyhood home, lay over one-million acres of wilderness and waterways; the Boundary Waters Canoe Area of northeastern Minnesota. Ray and his young companions had spent much of their free time inside the 'BWCA', eager to paddle their canoes over the exact same water routes of the early French Voyageurs. They would fish the same clear waters and camp on the same ancient sites the First People had used hundreds of years before. The rugged realm of the BWCA was the setting for their many open-air adventures.

This huge tract of land, once called 'the Great Roadless Area' had been protected and managed by the U.S. Forest Service since 1926. Through Acts of Congress, in both 1964 and 1978, the BWCA was established and designated a National Wilderness: "To remain forever preserved" in an unblemished and pristine condition. Add to that, the million-plus acres of Canada's Quetico Provincial Park, sister of the BWCA, and this unique, watery expanse more than doubled in size.

Long ago, centuries before the Native People settled here, the ever-expanding glaciers had punished this landmass, obliterating everything standing in the way of their gruesome and grinding path. Yet, when the last of the ice floes receded, after doing their worst, this good earth was rewarded two-fold for the pain and suffering inflicted. A primitive wilderness, as well as a matrix of sky-blue waterways was brought into being, from what was once a bleak, barren land.

Apart from a three year stint in the Army's Military Police, Ray had lived all of his thirty-three years here and he could think of no other place he would rather live out his life. Over those years, he had developed a close kinship with this rare backwoods area and it brought him great comfort to know that the water-laced refuge of his youth would never have to bear the heavy hand of civilization.

The light breeze that brought Ray the smell of the pines eventually worked its way through the thin Henley shirt he wore and triggered a momentary shiver. Although it was the third week of May, this far north the mornings were usually quite cool. Ray reached down and scruffed the neck of his two year-old Boxer pup, marking the customary end to his morning ritual. As he was about to turn and leave a movement off the end of the dock caught his eye. With barely a wisp of a watery murmur, a loon had surfaced a mere fifteen feet away, a large minnow clamped tightly in its' bill. In a quick, reflex motion, breakfast was swallowed. Ray froze in place, hoping not to alarm the normally shy bird. It was a rarity to see one this close up and he enjoyed the moment.

Years before, while out on the lake alone, he had witnessed a pair of loons swim just beneath his canoe. He still remembered how clearly he had been able to see the dark sheen of their iridescent-green heads and how stiffly they had strained their necks out ahead of their black and white checkered bodies; all the while using their wings as rudders. It had been but a fleeting glimpse of their swift, underwater flight for food, yet the image remained deeply rooted in him.

Ever alert and wary, the nearby loon slipped effortlessly back under the water only to materialize back into his view some thirty feet further away. Watching the sleek, fluid movements of the loon left Ray with an odd notion; that the lake itself resented the bird's early morning intrusion and had gently rejected the unwanted diver back to the surface. Ray smiled at the outlandish thought.

Angling away from him now, and low in the water, the bird turned a deep-red eye toward Ray and delivered a haunting cry across the lake. Far off and unseen, the loon's mate replied. To the unfamiliar, the wail of the common loon may well evoke a somewhat eerie, forlorn feeling. To Ray, the lonesome call was merely a reminder of how blessed he was to live and breathe in such an uncommon place.

Six years ago, Ray had built his cabin here, at the mid-way point of the peninsula his grandfather had purchased in 1922. He and his brother-in-law, Myron Jagunich, did the bulk of the construction work, splitting their time between home building and helping to run the family-owned resort business. Ray and 'Jag' took great care during the build, making sure they did not disturb the site any more than was necessary. The results were, the cozy, two-bedroom cabin had the look and feel of a home that had been here for many years. It nestled nicely into the pine-filled surroundings.

Thoroughly chilled, Ray shivered again and then spoke to his dog.

"Pretty nippy, Maggie. Feels like a two-shirt morning."

Ray stuffed his cold fingers deep into his pockets and stepped lively along the dock, back to his cabin, the dog at his heels. He went inside, put on a dark-blue sweatshirt and grabbed the keys to his old Ford Bronco. Halfway out the door, he stopped to look down at his worn jeans, making sure he had put on a clean pair. Clean enough, he decided. Ray rubbed his cheek as he hurried to the Bronco, realizing that he'd forgotten to shave again. No time left for that.

"Maggie. Truck." he said sharply.

The dog sprinted to the open tailgate and easily made the leap into the rear. She settled onto a heavy rug he had placed there for her.

"Good girl." Ray patted her head, "It's almost sunrise and I'm late again. Kyla's going to chew me out."

Minutes later he pulled alongside the main lodge of Lost Woman Resort & Outfitters, the business he and his family owned and operated. The resort, built along the base of Pike Point, lay on the outskirts of the BWCA and was one of the main 'jumping-off' points for people wanting to enter into the million-acre national park.

Ray took some time to feed and water Maggie, kenneling her when she finished. He made a quick scan of the rental cabins on either side of the lodge and was relieved to see that no early risers were out and about. He skipped over most the steps on the short flight of stairs leading to the private rear-entrance and then walked inside. The familiar smells of breakfast cooking washed over him as he made his way down the short hallway and into the kitchen. As expected, his mother Ellie stood at the front of the grill.

"I'm hungry, Ma!" he called out for the ten-thousandth time in his life.

"And a 'Good Morning' to you too, Ray," was her smiling reply.

"How about two eggs and some English muffins?"

Ray gave her a one-armed hug. Ellie, finishing a jellied muffin of her own, gave him a happy nod and turned back to the grill.

He poured a large orange juice from the kitchen's dispenser, drank most of it, and then refilled the glass.

"Kyla mad 'cause I'm late again?" he asked before draining the rest of his juice.

"Probably," Ellie answered. "But I believe she'll let you off the hook today. We've got a special guest for breakfast, so I don't think your sister will be too hard on you."

"Special guest?" Ray wondered aloud. "Who?"

"Go see for yourself."

Ray slowly opened one half of the tall, batwing doors and peeked into the lodge's dining room. There, seated at the head of one of tables, was his grandfather.

Paavo was ninety-three now. A life filled with constant work and clean living had helped keep him fit well into his advanced years, though his lean body was bent and had shrunken slightly from the burden of his years. The once sandy-colored hair was totally gray and his old face carried deep wrinkles from decades of outdoor living. But those light-blue eyes still held their twinkle and his mind was clear as a bell. His only concession to old age was a walking stick, never far out of reach.

Ray smiled at the sight of him, sitting there in his blue chambray shirt; the long sleeves rolled up just below the elbows, revealing the wrist-length arms of the white undershirt beneath. Although he couldn't see for sure, Ray imagined that his grandfather also wore his customary khaki-brown pants and a well-worn pair of lace-up boots. He'd hardly ever seen the old man wear anything different.

To simply label this special man 'Grampa' seemed, at certain times, inadequate. Throughout the years, it was Paavo's calm steadiness the family had always relied on; especially after Ray's father, John Maki, was killed in an automobile accident. And even though Paavo had lost his treasured son, it was in his firm, trusted grip that Ellie and the two children had placed their fears and uncertainties. Each of them had grieved individually, to be sure. Yet without Paavo, their heartache would have grown deeper and endured longer.

Paavo was seventy-three when his son died in that awful car wreck. An age, Ray had eventually come to realize, when most people turn to others for care and comfort. Nevertheless, his grandfather had stepped up quietly and confidently to become the family's lifeline. No words could express how much he admired and cared for the old man seated out there in the dining room. Whenever anyone told Ray how much he looked like, or reminded them of a young Paavo, a smile would appear on his face and a lump would lodge in his throat.

"If only that were half true," Ray always thought.

What Ray didn't realize, however, was when he looked over to his grandfather, he was really seeing himself, sixty years down the road. He had the same light-blue eyes and square, dimpled chin. He had the same lean and tightly-packed frame that Paavo had possessed in his youth. Ray also had a special quality that his grandfather had spoken of so often. Ray had 'sisu' - a Finnish term for a gutsy, determined spirit that was inborn and carried deep inside. That same inner-strength had served Paavo admirably, all through his long life.

And Ray knew the story of that long life because his father had made sure to tell him. John Maki had told his boy of a brave young man who, after losing his entire family, had chosen to come to America; eighteen years old and all alone, with but a trifle of money tucked into his shoe. And John had told of how Paavo and his young wife had suffered through the death of an infant daughter, only to be followed closely by the crushing load of a Great Depression. Wide-eyed Ray had listened intently when his father quietly spoke of how Paavo had become a widower while he, John, had been far away, fighting in a world war.

And then sadly, John too, had died.

Yes, Ray knew that life had struck full-force at his grandfather, many times. Yet here the old man was, clear-eyed and unbroken, the gentle owner of a strong spirit.

This was a special morning because any amount of time spent with this rare man was highly valued by everyone in the family, and none more so than Ray. Paavo seldom showed up at the resort anymore, preferring instead to stay close to home at the end of Pike Point, filling his days with countless, small chores of his own invention.

Ray continued to watch through the thin sliver of the door opening as the old Finn traditionally sipped his steaming coffee from the cup's saucer. His bony-knuckled, work-worn hands trembling slightly.

Behind Ray, someone came in the rear entrance he had used earlier. "Kyla," he said to himself after recognizing her footsteps. He felt it best not to turn around and say hello.

"I'm way better off not saying anything," he thought.

Ray hoped his sister would ignore his presence.

She did.

"How you be, Raymi?" Paavo asked, noticing his grandson in the nearly closed doorway.

"Nothing wrong with his eyesight," Ray thought as he entered the room. "Well, Grampa, I'm good and getting better. How are you today?"

"It hurts a little to be me this morning."

Ray grinned at the predictable answer.

"What brings you here?"

Paavo winked at his grandson and then spoke loud enough so the two women in the kitchen could hear him. His voice sounded very serious and sincere.

"I think I'm going to die today, Raymi. I come here to have one last meal with my lovely family."

Kyla popped her head out of the kitchen immediately, a worried look on her face. Ray waited for the full effect and then played along.

"You said the same thing at Easter."

"I know, I know," Paavo admitted. "I only say that so your Mama feel bad for me, then she give me another piece of pie. But this time, I know I be right."

Paavo continued, playfully now, as he looked directly at his granddaughter.

"Unless…maybe my Kyla will promise to bake me some cookies. Then I can wait one more day to kick the bucket."

Kyla shook her head back and forth in disgust. She disappeared into the kitchen, grumbling loudly to herself, not wanting to hear the two men chuckling.

Ray crossed the room and laid a hand gently on his grandfather's shoulder. He bent down, kissed Paavo on the temple and whispered in his ear.

"I love you, Grampa."

"You too, Raymi."

Paavo patted the back of Ray's hand and nodded ever so slightly, cherishing his grandson's words. Kyla witnessed the tender exchange and her irritation at the two jokesters melted away. She set their meals and a fresh pot of coffee on the table, a soft-hearted smile on her face. She gave her grandfather a kiss of her own.

"Your kisses, they are very nice, Kyla. But our Raymi, maybe he should save his kisses for the girls. Don't you think?"

Paavo winked at her this time. Kyla spotted the opening.

"Forget it, Grampa. I've totally given up on him. He's thirty-three years old and still single. I think he might be gay."

"What does this 'gay' mean?" Paavo asked, enjoying the game he'd started.

Kyla answered delicately.

"It means, you know, he doesn't, ahh…he doesn't go for girls."

"Oh no. That be true, Raymi? You don't like the girls?"

"I love women, Grampa. I just haven't been able to find one as pretty as Kyla."

A look of pure innocence formed on Ray's face.

"Schmoozer."

Kyla gave Ray's arm a playful jab. She suddenly got very serious, remembering she was trying to be mad at her brother for his late arrival.

"Sit down and eat your breakfast, Ray. I haven't got the time for all this bull. I've got to run upstairs and see if the boys are getting ready for school. *Unlike you*, they've already eaten."

Kyla hurried for the backstairs to check on her young sons. Paavo wasn't quite done.

"Kyla…I just think of something. Maybe our Raymi is not 'gay'. Maybe, he is like a rooster, and he likes *all* the girls, not just one."

The two men heard Ellie's laughter from the kitchen. Kyla turned back quickly, caught off guard again.

"Grampa! I'm surprised at you. That is just gross! And sexist!"

Kyla saw the impish grin appear on Paavo's face and her ire dissolved a second time. It was impossible for her to stay mad at him so she gave up and joined in. Imitating her grandfather's deep scowl and his Finnish accent, Kyla wagged an index finger in his direction.

"You always be full of the devil, Paavo Maki!"

Kyla bugged-out her eyes and stuck out her tongue, as she had done almost every day of her youth. She turned away in a flash and bounded up the stairs, leaving both men in stitches.

Seconds after Kyla disappeared, her husband came in the front door of the resort. Myron 'Jag' Jagunich was an imposing figure, at least three or four inches taller than Ray's six feet, and a good fifty pounds heavier. He was an easy-going kind of guy with a huge appetite for good food and hard work. Ray loved his unflappable nature along with his dry sense of humor. Jag walked over to the table and sat down across from Ray.

"Good morning, men," he said, taking off his cap and exposing a mop of dark brown, wavy hair. "Nice to see you, Grampa Maki. How's your love life?"

"Not so good, Jag," Paavo answered without hesitation. "I be down to only two girlfriends now. My number three girlfriend, she moves out of town."

"That's a real shame," Jag said sadly. "But don't take it personal. Lots of women leave town after finishing college."

Paavo snickered at the good humor.

"Don't you worry about me, I be okay. You save your worry for my grandson."

"Oh? Why's that?"

"Kyla, she thinks that Raymi doesn't like the girls."

Jag jerked his head toward Ray. He declared, "I'll be taking no more saunas with you, Maki!"

Paavo laughed until he had tears in his eyes.

Their light-hearted banter was interrupted by the loud slamming of an upstairs door. The high-pitched squeals of Kyla and Jag's two young sons penetrated their way throughout the lodge. Thankfully, Kyla got the shrieking to stop, but it was soon followed by a loud, rhythmic chanting and a purposeful pounding of little sneakers on the stairs.

"Ah!...Ah!...Ah!...Ah!" they uttered with every step down. Kyla herded them from behind them, shushing the noisy pair the whole way.

Then, two miniature, male-versions of Kyla burst into the room; Billy, the eight-year old, and J.P., age six. They were blonde and blue-eyed; good-looking boys that were full of life. They continued their chant as they circled the table where the three men sat. Jag sipped his coffee calmly, totally unruffled by the hubbub. Paavo looked to Kyla, hoping she would stop the mayhem. She only walked over, sat next to Ray, and heaved a surrendering sigh.

Ray stared at his sister. He knew what she was experiencing right now was some form of payback. As a young girl, Kyla had been the classic tomboy, following right alongside her older brother and his friends, copying everything they would do, trying to match them step for step. She had been a small female dynamo, on the go from sunrise to sunset. Their father, John, had called her Taz, after the Tasmanian Devil character. The nickname would stick, all the way through her teens. But when her head would touch the pillow at bedtime, she'd fall asleep immediately. Paavo would often comment, "Our little Kyla, she be like a light switch, either all the way on, or all the way off."

Finally, to everyone's relief, Ellie came out of the kitchen and corralled the happy hooligans. When they finished with their squirming, she lightly kissed the tops of their heads.

"You little sweethearts have a good day and make sure to behave in school. Okay?"

"We will, Gramma," they chimed together.

Kyla rolled her eyes at the remote possibility.

Jag stood up.

"Grab your backpacks and come with me boys. We're going outside to wait for the bus."

"Yippee! Skippee!"

They repeated it loudly, all the way out the door.

The four people left in the dining room sat in silence, enjoying the welcome quiet. After a few moments, Ray spoke to his sister.

"Hey, Taz. Do they remind you of anyone?"

Kyla saw zero humor in his question.

"It's barely a half an hour past sunrise and I'm already worn out," Kyla moaned. She looked to Ellie, hoping for a little sympathy. "I was never like those two demons. Was I Mom?"

Ellie simply replied, "Kyla, if you plant corn - you get corn."

Paavo and Ray nodded, in total agreement with the keen observation.

# 2

ANGIE HOLTER CHECKED HER WRISTWATCH before entering the examination room. Good, only eleven-thirty. With any sort of luck she'd be out of the clinic by noon and on a well-earned vacation. She slid the patient chart off the door, studied it for a little minute and walked in, closing the door behind her.

"Good morning, Mr. Dunstan. How's your knee healing up?"

Angie loved practicing medicine. She could think of no other career that would suit her better. Every aspect of the profession appealed to her natural instincts. Angie cared for people, and it always showed. She was happy, thankful to have found her niche in life.

Early on, at the beginning of nursing school, Angie knew she had found her calling. The demanding classroom training, the medical jargon and organized professionalism, even the antiseptic smells of her surroundings, all of it, only added to the initial fascination she'd had for her chosen field. Back then, the bigger the challenge in front her, the harder she had worked.

After graduation and finally able to make full use her acquired skills, medicine became a passion. For her, helping those who were in need of medical care was enormously satisfying work. And as a nice bonus, most patients she attended to were so grateful for even the smallest kindness she would show them. To Angie, nursing was a doubly rewarding career.

Nonetheless, as fulfilling and challenging as nursing was, Angie soon realized she could do more; for her patients and for herself. She continued on with her education until she received her Master's Degree in Nursing from the University of Minnesota; home to one of the most prestigious medical programs in the country. After passing all of the State Certifications, Angie obtained her license to practice medicine as a N.P., a Nurse Practitioner, which she had done for the past five years, here in St.Paul, at the Eagan Community Clinic.

But that was about to change.

Yesterday afternoon the CEO of the expanding clinic had turned Angie's world upside down by offering to her the newly established position of Nursing Director. The proposal had come as a complete surprise, given her age, but her boss had been insistent when telling Angie she had all the right credentials and would be the perfect person for the job. Angie was excited and honored, and had returned the surprise by asking for a private meeting with the Clinic Board before making any firm decision. She wanted more information, and would not be rushed, she had told him, the new job was much too important.

The Eagan clinic had a wide reputation for excellence and Angie knew the opportunity of a lifetime was in front of her, yet she had hesitated - for two very good reasons. First, and most important to her, Angie did not want to lose contact with her patients. They were the most rewarding part of her work. Secondly, hers was an already full schedule and she did not want it to become overwhelming. To her way of thinking, many more questions about the new Director's responsibilities needed to be answered, to her satisfaction. All the same, Angie was deeply flattered she had even been considered for the important post.

At quarter-to-twelve, Angie held the door open for good old Mr. Dunstan and his crutches. She dispensed her last bit of common sense advice.

"Glen, most people in the 'Over-Fifty' League don't slide into second base anymore. Next time, please be happy with a single. I'm sure your softball buddies will understand. Take care and I'll see you again in two weeks."

Angie was putting the finishing touches on the Dunstan chart when her nursing assistant tapped lightly on the door and walked in. Looking a bit frazzled, Kate blew out a deep breath and leaned the door closed with her back.

"This place is a total zoo. You better get your butt out of here before I find you another patient."

"Almost done," Angie said, scribbling down a few notations. "There. I am officially on vacation."

She handed the chart to her assistant.

"I am so jealous, Angie. I wish I could leave with you, but I guess I'm not as special as some people around here."

"Poor baby," Angie said, pursing her lips. "And don't be jealous, it's not like I'm planning to spend a month in Europe. I'm only going to visit my parents at their lake place for a few days."

"Take me with you," Kate pleaded. "I promise I'll try to behave."

"Sorry, I couldn't do that to my Mom and Dad. I actually like them."

Kate recovered quickly from the turndown, her eyes growing big.

"What did they say when you told them about the promotion?"

"I haven't said a word. Everything is too much up in the air."

"Too much up in the air? Are you serious, Angie?" Kate couldn't believe it. "Don't tell me you're thinking about turning down the job."

"I'm not convinced it's the best thing for me."

"More money, more benefits, more prestige, more everything. What's to think about?"

"More work, more hours, more pressure, less time for me," Angie argued back. "I need to work out a lot of the details before making a final decision. I guess this vacation couldn't have come at a better time. It'll give me some breathing room."

"I bet we'll hear your answer on Monday morning," Kate grinned. "When you're checking in to see if we've destroyed this place."

"Glad you mentioned it." Angie handed her a small note. "That's my parent's phone number, if you should need to get hold of me."

Kate frowned at the paper.

"This area code is different. What lake are they on?"

"I honestly don't know," Angie said. "I've never been there. It's some place way up in the boonies."

Kate still seemed puzzled so Angie offered more.

"About a year ago my Dad sold out his carpentry business. After he and Mom got rid of their house in Duluth, they retired to this lake place."

"So you're leaving here in less than an hour and you don't even know the name of the lake they live on."

"They've told me the name but I've forgotten it."

"That doesn't sound like you at all," Kate said skeptically. "Don't you think it might be kind of handy to find out where they live? You know, so you don't end up all alone, out in the middle of nowhere."

"I promise not to drive myself off the edge of the Earth," Angie grinned. "Besides, my Dad gave me some very simple directions. All I have to do is drive north about two hundred-fifty miles. When I get to the town of Ely, I keep on going. And just before the road ends, I turn left."

"Sounds simple enough. Maybe your Dad should come out of retirement and work for Triple-A Travel." Kate got serious when Angie stood up and took off her lab coat. "Anyway, Lord knows you deserve a bunch of time off. I hope you have a great time."

"Thanks, Kate. I really think I will, if I can forget about this place when I get there."

"I doubt that. Most workaholics like you can't turn it off."

"I thought you said I was a Type-A personality."

"You're both," Kate replied matter-of-factly. "You also have a slight touch of hyper-activity. Now that I think about it more, it will actually be a relief to have you gone for a while."

"Thanks for the warm, fuzzy send-off…Nurse Prickly."

They both laughed and gave each other an affectionate goodbye-hug.

Less than fifteen minutes later, Angie arrived at her home on Raspberry Lane, located in the quiet St. Paul suburb of Eagan. She backed her Camry into the driveway, fingered the remote for the garage door and popped open the trunk lid.

Angie shouldered her purse and grabbed the two freshly-packed suitcases she had put inside the garage earlier in the morning. She loaded them into the trunk, leaving the lid open. Back inside the garage, she pushed the wall button, closing the door behind her.

Once inside the house, she stopped at the dining room table and checked on the note she had left for the two nursing students who rented rooms from her. There, at the bottom of the long list filled with motherly instructions were drawn two smiley-faces, and a few words telling Angie not to worry, and to also have a nice time. She smiled back at the paper.

Angie was pleased that it had worked out so well to have a couple of energetic, younger females in the house with her. She truly enjoyed their company. Tina and Jessie were generally well-behaved, and to Angie's benefit, she was rarely left alone in the large house anymore. The girls often came to her for help with their nursing studies and both sets of parents felt much more at ease knowing their teenage daughters were living in a safe neighborhood and well looked after. The arrangement was a good one for all involved. Angie was grateful to her father for having suggested the idea.

She hurried to her private bath off the master bedroom and took a quick shower. She toweled off, covered up, then dried and styled her hair. After putting on a touch of fresh make-up, she slipped into a long-sleeved white blouse and a dark pair of tight-fitting jeans. Angie rolled up the cuffs of the blouse once and then wrapped the tails into the waistband of her pants. She put in a small set of fake emerald earrings and carefully latched the Cross necklace her parents bought for her last Christmas. Checking herself in front of the bedroom's full-length mirror, Angie turned left, then right, happy with the results. She slapped her rear once and said, "Not bad for almost thirty."

By any standards, Angie was a knockout. She was tall, nearly five-seven; and fit, with the right amount of curves in just the right places. She kept her naturally-wavy, auburn hair cut short to save time and fussing. It matched her face perfectly. Her full, well-manicured eyebrows arched themselves nicely over a set of big, beautiful green eyes - her best feature. Add to that a cute, lightly freckled nose and the whole effect was very appealing.

From the earliest she could remember her father would often say, "Tell me, Angie. What's prettier than a red-headed girl with green eyes?"

"What, Daddy?"

"Nothing, Angie. Absolutely nothing."

She hustled to the kitchen next, stopping again at the dining room table to get her keys, camera bag and purse. She opened the refrigerator door, grabbed a small bottle of pineapple juice and the bag lunch she had made before breakfast. She hurried to the front door, slid the proper key into the deadbolt, and then donned a light brown pair of beaded moccasins. Angie scooped up a tan leather case packed with her toiletries along with a black, well-supplied medical bag. Out the door she went, locking it behind her, despite having her hands full. She put the two cases into the open trunk and closed the lid firmly.

"There," she said, proudly looking at her watch. "Thirty-five minutes, start to finish. Don't tell *me* about Type-A personalities, at least we can get things done."

"What's that?"

Angie hadn't noticed her neighbor at his mailbox.

"Nothing, Hank. Just talking to myself … again."

"Welcome to my world." He added, "I saw you loading up your car. You told me you weren't leaving until Saturday morning."

"I made a break in my schedule so I'd be able to leave sooner. I'm hoping to surprise Mom and Dad by showing up today."

"Well, tell them Hank says hello."

"I will."

"I'll make sure to keep an eye on Tina and Jessie," he offered, pointing toward Angie's house.

"Thank you. I'd appreciate that."

She waved goodbye and ducked into the car.

Traffic was heavier than she anticipated, with much of it northbound like her, although it moved along quickly. Within thirty minutes she was out of the metro-area and heading north on the interstate. Angie did some rough math in her head while eating her bag lunch, concluding that she should be able to make it to her parents by late afternoon, possibly before dinner.

"I hope we can go out to a nice restaurant and have a peaceful, relaxing meal," she mused. "That would be a good time to tell them about the offer."

Her dinner idea got Angie to wondering if there were any good restaurants in Ely, or anywhere nearby.

"There must be," she decided, thus ending the short debate with herself.

Angie slid a well-used 'Boston' disc into the CD player and resisted the temptation to set the cruise control at eighty, settling instead on a safer, semi-legal seventy-five. The Toyota ate up the miles smoothly and soon the flat farmlands of southern Minnesota were left behind.

She stopped once, in Cloquet, a small city twenty miles west of her hometown of Duluth. Angie topped off the gas tank, used the restroom, and bought a yogurt bar to munch on. She looked at her watch for the hundredth time and remembered that Kate had pointed out to her, Type-A people did that sort of thing constantly. She dismissed the guilty thought, satisfied that, because of her efficiency, she would probably be able to have a pleasant, late afternoon meal with her parents.

An hour or so later, Angie spotted a road sign directing her to take the next right exit, toward Ely. This was new territory for her. She had never been this far north in the state. The next road marker informed Angie that she was now atop the Laurentian Divide, a very old and very unique geologic formation, if she remembered correctly from high school.

Soon the landscape changed dramatically. The road was no longer straight but full of twists and turns. Up hills, down hills, she curved around lakes and crossed over small rivers and streams. Exposed bedrock popped into view on either side and tall evergreens of all types crowded the shoulders of the road. She automatically slowed the car as her eyes took in the new scenery, no longer only focused on the highway ahead. A rustic, wooden signpost, lettered in yellow, confirmed exactly what she was feeling.

"Entering the Superior National Forest"

"No kidding," she whispered.

Sometime later, when Angie arrived in Ely, she did as her father instructed. She continued on, up through the steep mainstreet of the busy little town but not before taking notice of the many eye-catching craft stores and souvenir shops packed along the way.

"Mom and I are definitely coming back here."

A short distance outside of Ely Angie slowed her car again, aware that the asphalt surface had given way to a tight and winding gravel road.

"I must be getting close," she thought, turning off the music and pressing the down button for the window. She didn't want to miss the correct turn.

The age-old forest dominated everything. Huge pines shaded the entire road and pinched themselves so close; it caused Angie concern for the car's passenger-side mirror. All along the road's edge, the snake-like roots of the evergreens were exposed and appeared to be reaching out for more purchase into the soil of the narrow roadway. Even though the gravel and a thin layer of light-brown pine needles crunched quietly under her tires, Angie felt a hushed remoteness all around her. She drove on for several slow minutes as the alternating smell of pine and fresh water forced its way through the open window of the car. The whole area felt so secluded and isolated. The first-time feeling of having no other person nearby actually made Angie uncomfortable. The overpowering quiet was a completely new experience.

So consumed and distracted by the wildness all around her, Angie missed the turn-off to her parent's lake home. She drove on, through an easy, right-hand turn.

This was a totally different world when compared to the busy metropolis she'd left behind only a few hours ago. She was reminded of what Kate had said earlier; about ending up in the middle of nowhere.

Then, just as her father had said, the road ended.

# 3

A QUICK CUP OF COFFEE revived Kyla from the early morning drubbing she had received at the hands of her two energetic urchins. By the time the school bus had come and gone she was her old self again; ready to meet the busy day head-on. After Ellie escorted Paavo up to the second floor living quarters where Kyla and Jag made their home, the four of them met in the lobby of the resort. From behind a glass souvenir case that doubled as the check-in counter, Kyla handed a lengthy list of the day's duties to Ray and Jag.

"Typical Friday," she informed them.

"Yippee Skippee," Jag chirped.

Kyla was the driving force behind the day-to-day operation of the resort. Not only was she the chief organizer, she was also the head accountant and the resort's purchasing agent. She was an efficient manager who used her considerable energy to smoothly guide their thriving business. Kyla gladly accepted the wide range of demands her numerous jobs required and she took them very seriously.

During the past two off-seasons, Kyla had taken every computer class offered by the local community college and had recently purchased a brand-new, very expensive computer. Now she could take inventory, place orders, schedule camping reservations, oversee payroll and a hundred other things, all at the push of a few buttons. Much to the dismay of Ray and Jag, Kyla had also bought a state-of-the-art printer, a product of which, they now held in their hands.

Ray scanned down the detailed list of chores on the freshly printed page.

"You forgot to put down when I could take a leak."

"Go in your pants, smart guy."

Kyla had her game-face on.

"That'd be perfect, Maki," Jag jumped in. "Then you'd fit right in with the drunked-up Laurel and Hardy we've got staying over in Cabin Eight."

"I know who you mean," Ellie said in a half whisper. "I saw them yesterday, when they were checking in. Have they caused trouble already?"

"Some...last night around eleven o'clock," Jag answered.

"What kind of trouble?" Ray wanted to know.

"Loud music, rough language, that sort of thing. They were both pretty gassed up. The three of us had a nice little talk about not disturbing the other guests, and me. The smaller guy apologized right away, he knew I meant business. But his big buddy didn't say a word, he just sat there. I'm gonna have to keep a close eye on Stan and Ollie. They're not here for a nature-fest."

Ray wished he could have been there. He had seen Jag in action before, under similar circumstances. The big man was slow to anger but he could be very intimidating when pushed the wrong way. Jag was actually scary when riled-up and he was absolutely no one to mess with. If the two dirtbags in Number Eight had any smarts at all, they'd clean up their act, but quick.

Ray tried goading a stronger reaction out of Jag.

"I suppose I'll have to go over there and apologize for your terrible rudeness."

"Excellent idea. Please tell them I'm very sorry, and that I never meant to hurt their feelings."

Jag wasn't taking the obvious bait.

"Ahem," Kyla interrupted. "Okay, wise-guys, let's get back to the real world. We open the doors in a few minutes." She turned to Ellie. "All set on your end, Mom?"

"We're good for now, Kyla. Sometime before lunch, I'll get you an updated list of all things you'll need to order."

Ellie was the manager of the resort's restaurant. She set the menu, took reservations, and oversaw the kitchen and wait staff; along with meeting and greeting dining guests. She also maintained a close inventory on the wide variety of food and other items needed to keep the busy eatery functioning.

After the death of her husband, Ellie had proposed the idea of opening a restaurant on the first floor the main lodge. She had reasoned, instead of closing down the entire resort each fall, a good eating spot could operate year-round. Although it was a gamble, Paavo had agreed with Ellie's logic. He also understood her unspoken need to establish herself as the main breadwinner for her family - for fear that something terrible would possibly befall him.

So, after a long winters-worth of remodeling, the new restaurant opened its' doors in the spring of 1973. To Ellie's mild surprise and great relief, the well-run establishment rapidly became a popular place to gather. Not only did resort guests enjoy the high-quality food and good service, local people liked eating there as well. By the end of that season, the entire Maki family breathed a whole lot easier.

And Ellie was the perfect person to be in charge. Her cheery smile would crinkle up her compassionate eyes and somehow make you feel welcome. She had a pretty, round face with deeply-set dimples that appeared instantly on her cheeks whenever she did smile, which was almost all the time.

"Oh!" Ellie reminded herself, "Before I forget, later this afternoon Ray needs to bring Skinny his monthly supplies."

"No problem," Ray said quickly.

"Wouldn't want it any other way, Maki. The old goof kinda creeps me out."

Jag was more than willing to stay behind.

Skinny, was Skinny Severson; a short-tempered, self-imposed loner. A one-of-a-kind eccentric who lived in a single-room cottage that was located five or so miles east of the resort. The only access to his home was a tight, gnarly trail that had been plowed through the woods more than fifty years ago, to fight fires. Skinny eked out a meager living carving and painting perfect replicas of local waterfowl and upland birdlife. He also made Diamond Willow walking sticks and hand-crafted canoe paddles. All of his wares sold quickly at the local consignment shops in Ely, with Ray usually doing the legwork for him. A substantial amount of his earnings ended up in the vast whiskey coffers of the Seagram's family. The only companionship the quirky old man had, or wanted, was a brassy French bulldog named Bridget Bardot.

Ray carried the long list Kyla had handed him out to his truck. Making sure he couldn't be seen, he crumpled it up and threw it into the half-cab of his Bronco. He didn't need a roster to tell him what needed to be done but it made his sister happy to provide him with one. Ray bore no resentment against Kyla's take-charge style; on the contrary, he was more than glad she'd taken over the inner workings of the family business. It meant fewer headaches for him.

Ray opened the kennel door and let out a wriggling Maggie. He ordered her to sit, then commanded "Grampa", and pointed toward the

*Pike Point*

end of the peninsula. The young pup took off as if shot from a cannon; streaking headlong to where grandfather Paavo and mother Ellie lived, at the end of Pike Point. Most days, at the finish line of her carefree sprint, Maggie would find Paavo ready and waiting with a few scraps of food he'd saved from his own breakfast. As Ray watched her run from his sight, he felt a slight twinge of guilt run through him. Grampa wasn't home today. He was upstairs of the lodge. Hopefully, though, Ellie had remembered to leave a little treat on the porch steps for his pup. If not, Maggie would still have a great time in her futile attempts to chase down the speedy squirrels that also made their home on the Point. She would be gone for hours.

The morning sped by as Ray busied himself, tending to the various wants or needs of the many vacationers using the resorts facilities. He and Jag had a total of twelve rental cabins to look after, eight of which were strung along the east shore, and built on land purchased by John Maki after his return home from the Second World War. The remaining rentals, west of the main lodge, were larger and of the two or three-bedroom variety. These were the newest of the resort's buildings, built by his father and grandfather in the late 1940's and early 1950's. These updated cabins were meant for bigger groups wanting to enjoy the great outdoors, and who also felt the need for modern conveniences. The only exception was television, no cabin had a TV.

Ray and Jag's most important responsibilities were to make sure everything outside the doors of the main lodge was in proper working order. It was like being the landlords for twelve different and demanding households; with each one expecting, and deserving, prompt professional service. Add to that, the canoe and kayak rentals, along with the gear required. Hiking and back-packing equipment needed to be handed out. They also policed the tenting area and answered endless questions from well-meaning guests, all of it making for a semi-hectic, satisfying morning.

Around noon, Ray and his brother-in-law crossed paths for what seemed like the thousandth time.

"Man, I'm starving," Ray told him. "You hungry, too?"

"Since about ten minutes after breakfast. Come on, let's go grab a quick bite."

The two men made their way to the lodge and ate lunch together in the resort's kitchen. Jag was correct when he said "quick bite" because lunch never took him very long at all. Ray was constantly amused and always amazed at the sheer volume of food the brawny man could consume, in such a short amount of time.

Today would be no different.

While Ray ate a hearty helping of homemade chili and a hefty grilled-cheese sandwich, Jag managed to wolf down two bowls of his own, plus two robust, fish sandwiches. All of it down the hatch, in about ten minutes.

"That's it. I'm full," Ray declared, looking to his lunch partner.

He watched closely as Jag ate the final forkful from what was once a wide wedge of pumpkin pie.

"Don't you want your pie?" Jag stared at Ray in disbelief.

"Have at it, Hoss."

Ray slid his plate toward his smiling brother-in-law and watched as the big man squirted the entire top of the pie piece with a thick layer of whipped cream. Jag didn't bother with a fork or a plate this time. He picked up the dessert gingerly and in three enormous gulps, it was gone. Ray shook his head in wonder.

"What?!" Jag demanded, after swallowing hard.

"I didn't say anything," Ray answered calmly.

He was glad to see such a strong response from Jag.

"Don't go shaking your head like that. I'll tell you what, Maki. Maybe you'd have a big appetite too, if you worked for a living like me."

"You wanna know something, Jag? You are actually supposed to chew food. Twenty five times per bite, they say."

"You sure? I thought it was twenty five times per meal."

Jag let out a quick chortle, slapped the short countertop with a meaty palm and then walked down the hallway to the back entrance. Over his shoulder he hollered, "Follow me, Raymi-boy. And try to keep up this time."

He let out an evil, twisted laugh before disappearing out the door.

After lunch, time slipped away just as rapidly as it had in the morning. The busy pair had seven cabins to clean and prepare for newly arriving guests, all before the two o'clock check-in time. Surprisingly, they ended up with time to spare so they restocked the wood supply near each fire pit.

About mid-afternoon Ray made his way to the rear of lodge, checking to see if Maggie had returned from her patrol of Pike Point. He found her napping inside the open kennel, apparently worn down by her clever, uncatchable adversaries. He latched the door quietly.

Ray noticed someone had loaded five, well-stocked cardboard boxes into the back of his Bronco, nearly filling it. A month's worth of supplies destined for Skinny Severson. Ray recognized his mother's handiwork.

Ellie had a soft spot for Skinny, even though she rarely saw or had any contact with the old-timer. She always made sure that Skinny was taken care of, as much as the recluse would allow, anyway.

Ray entered the kitchen through the back door and spotted his mother sitting at the same counter where he and Jag had eaten their hasty noon meals. She was enjoying a cup of coffee, taking a short break from her restaurant duties. His mother didn't get much leisure time during her day and he hated disturbing her now. Sure enough, Ellie started to rise from the kitchen's stool when she saw her son. She reseated herself when Ray raised his hand.

"Don't get up, Ma. I just came in to tell you that I'm leaving for Skinny's place in a minute. Is there anything else I need to bring?"

"There's another small box for him in the cooler and here's the money from his last batch of sales." Ellie handed Ray a small envelope. "I was in town yesterday, so collected for him. I've already subtracted the money for his supplies."

Ray kissed his mother's forehead as he took the envelope. He knew any subtracting Ellie did from Skinny's scant income would be minimal. God love her tender heart.

"What was the kiss for?" Ellie asked with a big smile.

"You're too pretty not to kiss," Ray answered as he opened the cooler door. "You know, Ma? I was just thinking. I'm pretty sure you have a crush on Skinny. Why don't you ask him out on a date sometime?"

"I already have, many times," Ellie kidded back. "I must not appeal to him for some reason. Maybe it's because I still shave my legs. I guess I'm not continental enough."

Ray chuckled at the good joke and the unwanted picture it brought to mind. He closed the cooler door with his foot and slid the box under one arm. It was loaded to the top with multi-shaped, well-sealed, plastic containers. He envied Skinny for the cookies, cake pieces, and other sweet goodies he knew were inside the care package his mother had put together.

"If you keep this up, Skinny will have to change his name to Fatty."

Ellie shooed her son out the door with a wave of her hand.

Half an hour later Ray stopped the Bronco just past the half-way point of the five mile trek out to Skinny's, happy to be away from the resort for a while. Unlike Jag, he found the crusty old guy quite likeable, once you got through his intentionally gruff exterior. The old grump had an unusually tight circle of people he actually tolerated and Ray was one of them. Skinny was a particularly fascinating character who never failed to capture Ray's interest with his carving skills, or his peculiar personality.

Skinny was also an avid historian and had acquired a highly detailed knowledge of Ray's favorite subject; World War Two. Ray's father had served as paratrooper during those years and Skinny always held Ray's rapt attention whenever he spoke of those soldiers' grave sacrifices and their exceptional bravery.

"Your father," Skinny had once told Ray, "was one of the men who helped save the world."

And each time, following those drawn-out sessions, Ray had always walked away with a strong sense of pride, steeped in the knowledge that his father had played such a vital part in the winning of the war effort.

Ray stripped off his sweatshirt and gave permission for Maggie to exit the cramped quarters of the truck's box. The tightly-coiled dog catapulted herself over the side so quickly, and with such absolute abandon, he laughed out loud. Amazingly, she landed on all fours and was instantly on the track of some unsuspecting woodland creature.

"Stick around," Ray instructed.

The young Boxer seemed to understand and she crisscrossed her way along the rough trail a short distance in front of the slow-moving truck. As Ray weaved and bumped along, he reached over and picked up a pie-shaped Tupperware container his mother had left on the passenger seat. Ellie had even taped a plastic fork to the lid. He was hoping for a thick slice of blueberry.

It was.

Ray drove while eating, trying not to lose any tasty crumbs from the homemade snack. He finished up by washing it all down with a can of ice tea taken from the kitchen's cooler. Ray stopped the Bronco once again, in a low, swampy swale next to a natural clearing. Across the way he could see the slow-motion spins of the windmill his father and grandfather had helped Skinny erect many years before. It powered a small water pump, enabling the aging loner the simple comfort of indoor plumbing. The turning mill also served as a charging unit for a bank of batteries used in the lighting of his living quarters; an ingenious system designed entirely by Skinny himself.

Next to the truck, Maggie drank from the sluggish stream, panting between noisy gulps. She did a quiet belly flop into the shallow water, a large, drool-dripping grin on her face.

This was Ray's kind of afternoon; a nice, slow cruise through the quiet backwoods on a warm spring day. There was no one around to pester him and there were no concerns about his work being done on time. The only thing that lie ahead was an interesting and probably-amusing conversation with a very unique man.

But Ray's good feeling was slightly spoiled by something Kyla had said, not long ago. She laid bare the fact that Ray spent too much of his spare time alone and that he seemed to enjoy being away from people.

"You're going to end up like Skinny," she had warned, "just you and a stupid dog."

Ray pondered over his sister's grim prediction for his future. After only a few seconds, he decided that Kyla should tend to own business. Besides, she always worried too much, about everything.

He drove up a slight rise, wound around Skinny's unplanted vegetable garden, and parked alongside the compact, neat-as-a-pin cottage. The small building looked exactly the same as it did twenty-five years ago when he had first visited here with his father. The narrow-lapped siding was shiny white and the trim boards were painted in dark green. The only window of the dwelling faced south, looking out into the clearing.

All along the north end of the spacious, well-tended yard was row after row of perfectly stacked and split firewood, the old man's only source of warmth against the bitterly-cold Minnesota winters. Carefully piled alongside the west wall of the house were dozens of hand-sawn logs of varying length and diameter. The cut wood was raised off the ground and covered in heavy canvas, drying slowly, awaiting its' chance to be whittled into carbon copies of local birdlife.

Surrounding all of the yard's borders were densely packed Balsam Firs, a naturally fragrant windbreak. The tall trees served double duty by also providing cool shade during the hot months of mid-summer. It was obvious to the knowing eye that the tidy little home had not been placed in this spot by accident.

There was no sign of Skinny or his little dog, but that was nothing unusual. Many times Ray had come and gone without ever seeing either of them. He hoped the old man was nearby and had heard his arrival so they could have an entertaining chat. Ray carried the first box inside and set it on the floor near a well-organized washstand that was situated below the window. He turned to retrieve another load.

"Good afternoon, Mr. Maki."

Ray jumped, badly startled.

"Gees, Skinny! You scared the crap outta me!"

"Let us hope your statement is simply not true."

The old hermit sat in a high-backed leather chair placed near the room's center, its' back turned toward Ray.

"I am genuinely sorry," Skinny quickly added. "Frightening you was unintentional."

Something was amiss. There was no yapping coming from Bridget and no move from Skinny to get up off the chair. Ray peered into the dim, unlit living area where the old man sat but he failed to see much of anything.

"Where's your dog at?" Ray inquired, still trying to see into the shadows.

"Never end a sentence with a preposition," Skinny instructed. "Bridget is well and resting comfortably on the bunk."

After hearing her name, the little bulldog gave a quick yip.

"What's goin' on, Skinny?"

"In keeping with your opening remark, at this very moment in time, I partake in a rather large bite directly consumed from the shit sandwich of life."

Ray had no idea what was meant by the statement but it was a classic Skinny-type answer.

"Sounds like he's been drinking," Ray thought, although puzzled at the idea.

He knew that Skinny drank more than his fair share of Seagram's whiskey, as a matter of fact; there were two more bottles for him in the back of the truck. But Ray had never so much as seen him take a drink of the stuff. He'd always assumed the old guy saved that habit for the evening hours. Ray went out to retrieve another load. Once back inside, set the second box next to the first.

"Do you mind if I turn the lights on? It's pretty dark in here."

"If you feel you must," was the subdued reply.

"Definitely drunk," Ray concluded.

He flipped the light switch, then watched Skinny reach overhead and click off the single light bulb that dangled above his chair. Ray finished carrying in all of the supplies, leaving the special parcel Ellie had packed for last. He ordered Maggie into the truck box and re-entered the house.

"Ma's sent a bunch of goodies for you and here's the money left over from your sales."

"Your mother…a wonderful woman who bears the endless burden of a caring heart. Make sure to thank her for me, will you please? You may lay the cash on the wash stand."

"Can do."

"Now that, sir, is an incomplete sentence."

With the lights turned on, Ray could see clearly into the room. A large, pot-bellied stove stood near the corner bunk where Bridget rested, on top of a thin, red-blanketed mattress. The stove's door faced to the sleeping area so the old man could reload wood into it without having to completely leave the bed's warmth on cold nights. The walls and the low ceiling of the entire house were covered in beautifully finished, knotty-pine paneling. There were six tall and hand-crafted bookcases spaced along three of the walls. One-half of the cases were filled with volume after volume on the biographies of famous historical figures. The rest of the shelving was dedicated to books written about the Revolutionary and Civil Wars, along with other works relating to World Wars One and Two. There were many other textbooks on American and World history. It was an impressive collection.

The living area was neat, clean and well kept. On top of the bookcases, and in between them, the wall space was filled with striking examples of Skinny's craftsmanship. From where Ray was standing, the room could have passed for an outdoor-gentleman's private den from a bygone era. Except for one thing; the heavy workbench placed in front of the old-timers' chair.

Clamped to the edge of the squat table was a nearly finished, half-scale carving of a loon. The unpainted bird appeared to be permanently caught in an aggressive posture as it rose up from the table, wings spread, chest puffed out. The neck arched defiantly and its sharp, sturdy bill was pointed at a downward angle, toward an imaginary foe. The old artist had captured the pose perfectly. The vivid detail was astonishing.

"The loon is awesome, Skinny."

"I thank you, kind sir. The wings are not yet permanently mounted. I needed to determine if they were properly placed and in proportion to the body."

"I've never seen you do wings like that. They're incredible."

"I thank you once more, for the gracious compliments."

Ray resisted a strong urge to say a quick goodbye. It was obvious that Skinny was not his normal self and Ray didn't like being around anyone who'd had too much to drink. He'd already seen his full-ration of half-drunk men when he was in the army. Instead of leaving, though, Ray took an old crate from under the wash stand to use as a chair and set it down across from the workbench. As he bent down to sit, he looked over to the old man. What Ray saw jolted him upright.

"Skinny! You're hurt!"

"You have an uncanny grasp of the obvious, Mr. Maki."

The right side of Skinny's face was cut up and badly scraped, and he gazed up at Ray through large, watery eyes. The white area of his right eye was alarmingly darkened with ruptured blood vessels. His thinning, light-colored hair was combed back over the ears and his face held a heavy, two-day growth of white whiskers. The old man was truly thin but he seemed even more so now, clad in a sleeveless white undershirt that revealed his angular shape. A pair of reading glassed rested near the tip of his slightly long, redder-than-normal nose. Skinny stroked his neatly-trimmed walrus moustache with the thumb and forefinger of his left hand, in between short sips of whiskey. He was slumped low in the chair and a biography of Harry Truman lay unopened on his lap.

"What happened?!" Ray interrupted before Skinny could reply. "And your arm! Look at your arm!"

Skinny's right arm was wrapped in a make-shift bandage; made from a thin, cotton dishtowel, now heavily stained with blood. Deep, nasty-looking gashes were visible above and below the edges of the cloth. The flesh all around the cuts was a flushed, reddish color and Ray could see that some sort of ointment had been applied to the wounds.

"What happened?" Ray repeated in a calmer voice, finally sitting down.

"I was felling an old Basswood tree needed for future carvings. As the tree began to topple I heard a loud, cracking sound above my head. I looked up only to discover a widow-maker bearing down on me. There was little time to get out of the way…I ought to have known better." In a quoting voice, Skinny added, "The body often suffers, when the mind is weak."

Widow-makers. Ray had heard the term used by local loggers. It was the dead, top portion of a tree that would snap off as it fell, usually because its' branches were entangled with those of a close-growing neighbor. He'd been told these types of accidents had seriously injured or even killed more than a few wood cutters.

"When did this happen?"

"I am near to completing my second day of bliss."

Skinny raised his glass, as if offering a toast. He drained the small amount of whiskey left.

"I gotta tell you. This looks real bad. Can I…May I look your arm?"

Ray mistakenly thought he had spared himself another grammar lesson.

"The injuries appear far worse than they actually are. You may stand there and look at my arm for as long as it pleases you. However, you may not *examine* it…Doctor Maki."

Ray tried to ignore this latest correction but Skinny was being a real smartass, and it was getting frustrating. He also had enough of the superior attitude.

"Will you knock it the hell off?!"

Bridget growled a warning from the bunk.

Ray calmed himself, taking into consideration that the old man was mostly polite and had never spoken to him like this. He let out a short sigh before continuing.

"Are you in a lot of pain? Your arm is very red, and it looks infected."

Skinny too, changed his manner.

"The pain is bearable. As you can see, I am self-medicating." He tipped the empty glass in Ray's direction. "A tumbler of Seagram's works much better than any product Tylenol puts out on the market and the side effects are most pleasant…Now, as far as any infection is concerned; I cleansed the arm cuts thoroughly and rubbed an antibiotic cream over the entire area, as a precaution. I thank you for your concern, Ray. Let me assure you, there is no need for any worry on your part."

"I am worried, Skinny. What about your eyeball? What if that gets infected? Did you rub antibiotic cream on that?"

Skinny raised himself upright in the chair and leaned forward. Ray could see by the change in body language that the old man was nearing the limits of his tolerance.

"That, Ray, is enough talk about me."

Skinny paused. He held his battered eyelid closed with a fingertip and glared as best he could at Ray. He opened the book on his lap, tapping the pages in a clear attempt to change the subject.

"Would you care to hear a Harry Truman quote?"

"Right now, I don't care what Truman said."

"Never trust any preacher who owns more than two suits." Skinny said, not needing the book. "Now there is a simple statement that has stood the test of time. The man was a plain-speaking genius…Do you not think so?"

This was the first time Skinny had ever asked Ray for an opinion.

"What I think, is that you are hurt and seem to be in a lot of pain. You can't stop blinking. You need to go see a doctor."

He looked Skinny straight in his good eye.

The old man suddenly stuck out his tongue and blew a wet, New York-style raspberry at Ray and his medical opinion. It was Skinny's trademark; his way of punctuating an end to any unwanted debate. Ray had witnessed this before. Their conversation was clearly over.

Ray stood up, not saying a word. He picked up the crate he'd been sitting on and put it back under the washstand. He turned and spoke to the back of Skinny's chair.

"I'll be back in a day or two, to check on you. If your eye and your arm haven't improved, I *will* be taking you to see a doctor. And I don't care if I have to drag you out the door, kicking and screaming."

"Bring friends, Mr. Maki. You will need them."

An even louder raspberry followed Ray out the door.

The entire way back to the resort Ray tried convincing himself that Skinny would be fine. That he was a tough old codger. "Maybe I overreacted," he second-guessed. Or maybe the old fart was right, the injuries looked worse than they really were. After all, hadn't Skinny survived very nicely on his own, for many years? Wasn't it his choice to refuse help? And didn't he have a right to his own privacy?

All those worrisome thoughts and unanswered questions niggled at Ray for the entire trip home. They kept rolling through his mind, over and over, never quite finding a place to settle. He kept picturing Skinny sitting all alone in his dark, too-quiet house, with no one to talk to, except for a little black and white dog. He couldn't stop seeing the old man's sad face; all cut up and scratched, looking back at him.

In the end, Ray resolved to do exactly what he had promised. He would check on the stubborn old coot in a day or two. Maybe he'd even bring big 'ole Jag with him, for backup. But just the thought of interfering in Skinny's private life, and the big upset it would cause, unsettled his thoughts further. He hoped it didn't have to come down to that sort of unwanted ruckus.

Ray was about to turn off the road and park alongside the lodge when he spotted Jag and the boys slowly walking in his direction. The two youngsters looked unhappy and tired. There was no hint left of their early-morning enthusiasm. And Ray knew why.

Each boy carried an empty garbage bag as they went on their sad way to pick up litter and empty out trash cans from the resort's tenting area. Their next stop would be the gut shack, where guests could clean and fillet fish. This was the usual punishment imposed on them for any known misdeed, or bad conduct. Ray had seen this gloomy parade before, quite often.

He pulled off the edge of the road, crowding hard against the flexible branches of a White Pine sapling. He had long since quit caring about the truck's twenty-five year old paint job. Ray turned off the ignition and put an elbow out the open window, speaking to his nephews when they neared.

"Trouble?"

The guilty pair stopped and said nothing. They stared down at the tips of their sneakers. Jag spoke for them.

"These two desperados will be riding at the front of the bus for the rest of the school year. Right boys?"

There was no answer from Billy or J.P.

"The bus lady had a little chat with Kyla. I guess she doesn't appreciate anyone setting sparrows free inside the bus. At least, not while she's driving."

The boys risked a sideways glance at one another, trying very hard to stay sad-looking and not smile at the chaos they'd created on their wild ride home from school.

Jag waved them on.

"Alright you two hoodlums, get started."

After the boys were out of earshot, Ray offered an observation.

"I seem to remember someone showing them how to catch birds. A cardboard box, a few seeds, some string."

"I told them they had to let everything go, right away," Jag confessed quietly. "Oh man, please don't say anything to Kyla. I'll never hear the end of it."

"Poor kids," Ray rubbed it in. "Look at 'em, Jag. They look like somebody took away their birthdays."

"Poor kids my eye. Watch this…Hey boys! If you both do a real good job, maybe we'll have time for a wrestling match after supper."

Then instantly, out of nowhere, an unknown, invisible force entered the bodies of the two lads, causing their backs to stiffen sharply, compelling them to stare bug-eyed at one another. Within seconds, they went about their work with a totally renewed outlook, whispering and plotting a plan of attack; eager for the happy chance to tussle with their oversized father. It was the favorite pastime for all three.

Normally, Ray would have gotten a good chuckle after seeing the boys' abrupt transformation. He just sat quietly in the truck, wanting no part of the conversation he knew was about to take place. After Jag turned back in his direction, Ray had no choice.

"Skinny got hurt, Jag. A widow-maker fell on him."

"How bad?"

"Pretty bad, I think. Well, it looks bad. He wouldn't even consider going to see a doctor. Claimed there was nothing to worry about. But he was half in the bag trying to numb the pain. I could see that he was still hurting."

"What are you gonna do?"

"I don't know for sure. I guess I'll go back in a day or two." Ray looked away from Jag. "If he's no better, I told him that I would force him to come in."

"Ha! Good luck with that." Jag lightly slapped Ray's arm and started off in the direction his sons had taken. "I almost wish I could be there to see the old nutcase go ape-shit."

"Actually, I was hoping you'd come with me."

Ray winced when Jag stopped short. The big man retraced his few steps back to the truck and put both hands on the roof edge of the Bronco's half-cab. He leaned in, real close; to make sure he was heard.

"No stinkin' way, Maki. I told you a long time ago that I'm not goin' out to that screwball's place ever again."

"He's not a screwball, Jag."

"Oh really. You know yourself, the one time I went out there with you, all he did was give me the evil eye. He never so much as said, 'Hi', 'Goodbye', or 'Kiss my ass' to me...As far as I'm concerned, that qualifies him as a screwball."

"Skinny does that kind of thing on purpose. Once you really get to know him, he's no different than anybody else."

"Yeah, right. That's why he lives out in the middle of the woods, all by himself, because he's so normal and stable." Jag was getting wound up, talking louder now. "Answer me this Ray, how many sane people do you know that stick out their tongues and blow mouth-farts every ten minutes?"

"Do I get to count Billy and J.P.?"

Ray tried smiling the question. Jag wasn't amused, so Ray tried a white lie.

"Skinny has mellowed out quite a bit since the last time you've seen him."

"Oh sure thing, Maki. I ain't buyin' that load of freshly made-up bullshit…Another thing, tell me why anyone would want all those goofy books he's got on Nazis, and Hitler, and Mussolini. You told me that he's even got a book about that lunatic in Africa. The guy who ate people."

"Idi Amin?"

"Yeah, that sweetheart…And aren't you the fella who tells me he's always readin' about black plagues, and bloody massacres, and world wars? Only gun-totin' wackos read that kind of crap."

"I've never seen him with a gun," Ray countered feebly.

Jag was well past listening.

"And now that you went and pissed him off, you want me to go out there. Well, that's not gonna happen, Ray. I'll bet you dollars against dog turds that the old crackpot has already loaded up a friggin' bazooka, and he's just waitin' and prayin' for you to come back. Sorry pal, count me out. He's loopy."

"Skinny's a good man, Jag. You know damn well I wouldn't ask unless I thought he really needed help."

Jag could see that Ray was serious. They stared at each other for several long seconds.

"Damn it, Maki…If it was anybody else doing the asking."

"Well, I'm the guy asking."

"Okay then."

Jag pushed himself away from the truck, intentionally rocking it, and the driver. He walked away shaking his head and grumbling loud enough to make sure Ray could hear him.

"Widow-maker my ass. That half-baked oddity will probably make a widow out of your sister."

Ray leaned his head out the window.

"Thanks. And trust me, it won't be that bad."

Jag turned back and presented Ray with his third, and loudest, raspberry of the day.

Ray sat in the truck for a long time, brooding.

"Wonderful," he said out loud.

That made two people ticked-off at him; two people he really liked. He felt torn between trying to help his old friend Skinny and then having to impose on Jag's friendship.

"I should have left well-enough alone."

The more he thought about it, the more Ray felt like he'd jumped the gun with Skinny. He wished now that he had just kept quiet and not forced the doctor issue. His best bet would have been to show up at the old man's place in a couple of days to see how he was doing, then decide if anything needed to be done. He regretted how he had mishandled the whole mess. And things hadn't gone so well with the usually good-natured Jag. This was definitely not turning out to be the nice, pleasant afternoon he'd been expecting.

Ray nodded when he remembered what his grandfather had tried to teach him years ago, about giving some thought to a problem, before rushing ahead and making a bad situation worse. He quietly quoted Paavo to himself.

"It be too late to squeeze, Raymi, after the shit is in your pants."

Maggie barked loudly, as if agreeing. She only wondered what the holdup was.

"Sorry girl."

As Ray reached over to start the Bronco, a car pulled up tightly alongside him, its' passenger window sliding down.

"Excuse me. I think I may be a bit lost."

Ray looked down into the lower profile car to see a woman leaning over the center console. She stared up at him with the prettiest set of green eyes he had ever seen. And yet, he'd seen those same eyes before… somewhere. It took only a fraction of a second for him to remember.

"You're looking for the Holters."

The woman's eyebrows skirted up her forehead, forcing her big eyes to grow even bigger. The most charming, surprised look showed up and stopped itself on her face. Ray said nothing, hoping she'd keep it there for a while. Instead, she straightened up and out of his view.

When she leaned over in Ray's direction again, a whole new set of features frowned back at him, looking every bit as delightful as the first set he had seen just seconds ago.

Ray waited to hear what she had to say.

"How could you possibly know that I'm looking for the Holters?"

"You look like your mother." Ray amended the statement quickly, "Except for the hair."

Lois Holter had near-perfectly white hair. She also had the exact same eyes he saw in front of him. Ray hoped he hadn't offended her in any way and he grew a little nervous. He slid more upright in his seat.

"If you'll pull up further, so I can get out, I'll give you directions to your parents' place."

Ray tried hard to think of her first name as she drove her car forward. It wouldn't come to him. He got out of his truck when he was able, rubbing his chin as he walked around the backside of her car. He wished he had taken the time to shave this morning - and the morning before that. The thoughts "too late now, Raymi" entered his head but they disappeared from his mind after seeing the car's pretty driver again. He held out his hand in a half-greeting, half-apology.

"Ray Maki. Sorry about surprising you like that."

She smiled a perfect smile back at him while shaking his outstretched hand. He had to make a conscious effort to let go.

"Nice to meet you, Ray Maki. No need to apologize. I guess I wasn't expecting anyone here to know me."

"I've been to your folks' cabin a few times. Your mother has shown me a lot of your pictures. They both speak of you all the time."

She seemed slightly embarrassed.

"Oh no. But that does sound like them. It makes me wonder what else they've said."

"Well, they've mentioned your name, only I can't remember it right now."

"Angie."

"Right, Angie."

He liked saying the name...the name seemed fit her...man, those eyes. Ray smiled. He was fairly sure that it was his turn to speak but no words rolled out of his mouth. His next sentence was nowhere to be found, lost somewhere in his vacant head. The silly-ass grin on his face suddenly felt idiotic. Barely two seconds passed when Ray was seized by a moment of pure panic, realizing that his brain had gone into total vapor-lock. Ray frantically groped around in the dark emptiness that had once housed his mind - nothing there. He was deeply grateful when Maggie whined loudly from the back of the truck. Ray grasped at the straw handed to him by his dog.

"My dog would like to meet you," he said, extremely relieved to hear his own voice again. "C'mon girl."

Bad idea. Ray's mind remained mostly blank and now he felt like a tongue-tied third grader at show-and-tell. As his uneasiness grew, he came to the conclusion that it was probably best to remain quiet and hope she would do most of the talking. That way it would take her a little longer to figure him for the local idiot.

Angie got out of her car and purposely made a big fuss over an excited Maggie. The short delay bought Ray some time to locate a few of his missing thoughts and arrange them into some kind of rational order. He was about to offer his best attempt at giving Angie the directions she wanted when Billy and J.P. went skipping by.

"Uncle Ray's in luh-uv. Uncle Ray's in luh-uv."

Angie watched closely as the pint-sized agitators chanted loudly, in unison, all the way to the resort. Ray felt his face grow warm and red. He wanted to stuff the tiny trouble-makers into the half-empty, fish-gut garbage bags they were swinging around their heads. Jag passed near the car and added his two cents.

"Pesky neighbor kids. Are you almost ready for supper, Raymi?"

He'd put an emphasis on the nickname. Ray glared back at him as he walked past, sorry for the fact that Jag was way beyond being crammed into any plastic bag.

"I'll be there in a minute, Myron."

Ray received some mild satisfaction when he saw Jag give a slight hitch. He had never liked the name.

"Cute boys," Angie said. "Too bad they belong to the neighbor people."

Angie appeared unconcerned by it all and Ray sensed she was trying to ease his discomfort. He relaxed somewhat when he saw her understanding grin.

"My nephews. They're actually pretty good kids, when they're asleep."

"And who's the big kid?"

Ray laughed. "You couldn't be more right. That's my sister's husband, Myron Jackassovich…I mean, Jagunich."

While she giggled at Ray's old gag, he looked past his one-liner, at her again. Her laugh seemed to come easily and he was sure it was genuine.

For a second time, he had to make a conscious effort to release himself from her natural charm. This woman standing next to him seemed to have the baffling knack of disturbing his normally well-composed train of thought. He tried once more to give her the directions she wanted but Angie spoke first.

"It's so beautiful here, isn't it? All of the pine trees and the lake, the fresh air. It's wonderful." Ray kept his eyes on her as she took in the setting. "The old lodge fits in perfectly over there, doesn't it? And look at all those windows with a view out onto the lake. It all looks so…so fitting. It's like everything has been here forever."

"Well, not quite. The oldest part of the lodge was built in 1925, by my grandfather. He and my Dad expanded things after that."

Ray was proud to tell her a little family history.

"Do you own all this?" she asked in a surprised way.

"My family and I own it."

"It's a really lovely spot. Your father and grandfather did a remarkable job. It's gorgeous here, like something out of a picture book."

That was it for Ray. She couldn't have said anything more perfect if she tried. He looked into those beautiful green eyes and had to tamp down on an irrational impulse to kiss her cheek.

"Thank you," Ray said quietly.

Angie gave a glance down the road and another at her wristwatch. Ray took the unintended hint and finally offered the way to her parents' home.

"As you go back through that last curve, look in your rear-view mirror. Just after you lose sight of the lodge, you'll see a small road on the right. That road will take you to your parents' cabin. It's actually their driveway."

Ray's afternoon troubles were totally forgotten, his poor frame of mind had vanished. He continued to stare down the road long after the taillights of Angie's car disappeared from view. After a time, he turned at the sound of his grandfather's quiet approach.

"Raymi, why do you stand in the middle of the road like a wooden Indian?"

Ray's good humor lifted even more after seeing his grandfather. He laughed at the stationary image of himself, and at the old man's cutting wit. When Paavo got close enough, Ray gave him the one-armed hug usually reserved for his mother.

"Would you want to have supper with me, Grampa?"

"That would be a nice thing. Do you want to eat out here in the road?"

Ray saw the devilish glint in his grandfather's blue eyes. And the old man was trying his best to stifle a growing grin. Apparently, Grampa had been watching him for a while.

"Let's go eat supper, you old Finlander…Inside. Come on, Maggie."

Ray laid his arm across his grandfather's sniggering shoulders and the two fond friends walked slowly to the resort.

# 4.

Perhaps it was the longer traveling time. Or maybe it was her reaction to the secluded, unfamiliar surroundings. Whatever the reason, Angie's sunny mood clouded over as she drove down the narrow lane leading to her Mom and Dad's new home. She felt an odd detachment from them, as though no longer an important part of her parents' changed lives. Strangely, the closer she got to her destination, the further away she felt. The unexpected melancholy was troubling. She had wanted to feel happy.

In truth, Angie was feeling guilty about not seeing her Mom and Dad in such a long while, knowing that her busy life was mostly to blame. The last time they'd gotten together was in December, for the holidays. And now that she was considering an even heavier demand of her life, it seemed their lengthy separations would only continue, or possibly get worse. As Angie's once-cheerful outlook took a steady nosedive, the big news about her pending promotion didn't seem so important any more.

Without realizing, Angie reached up and tugged at her Cross necklace. Right now she didn't know how to resolve the situation. She only knew that she didn't want her parents to become only occasional guests in her life. They meant too much. It was then Angie decided the news of the offer could wait, for now. She'd tell them when the time felt right.

Before she stopped at the end of the circular turn-around, Angie saw the familiar signs of her father's carpentry trade everywhere. Yellow scaffolding spanned one length of the smallish, un-sided home, the old boarding already having been discarded. There were blue, tarp-covered stacks of construction materials piled all around the shady yard and Angie could see a screened-in porch had been added to one end of the house. The addition faced west, with a clear view of the nearby bay. In the center of the driveway loop, tri-colored landscaping blocks had been laid out in ringed tiers, waiting for the frosty mornings to end so they could be filled with topsoil and flowers. A wooden post had been driven down into the center of the tiers and a scalloped-edge sign that read 'Lois and Jim' hung from a wrought iron support. For a brief moment, Angie wished that her name was on it.

She spotted her father's quick appearance in a newly-framed window and before she could remove her baggage from the car, he was out the porch door and giving her a big hug.

"Ah, Rose, it's so good to see you."

The rare use of her middle name tinked an agreeable note in Angie's ear. Only Dad referred to her in that way and it was especially nice to hear the name again. Angie returned his strong embrace, hoping that he wouldn't let loose of her too quickly. After the right amount of heart-warming seconds, he pushed her out to arm's length and examined her face. Jim captured his daughter's heart with his fatherly approval and then pulled her close again, kissing her forehead lightly.

"Tell me, Angie. What's prettier than a red-headed girl with green eyes?"

Angie's eyes brimmed immediately and she was unable to play her part in their old routine. She quickly gave her Dad a second hug and then managed to squeak out, "I missed you, Daddy."

Jim hugged her back, not minding the unfinished game.

"You surprised me, kiddo. Mom and I weren't expecting you until sometime tomorrow. Matter of fact, she's not home right now, but I expect her soon."

"I got out of the clinic early. I couldn't wait to see you guys."

She reached down to pick up the suitcases but Jim beat her to it. Angie took the lighter cases out of the trunk and they carried her bags to the house, setting them inside the porch door.

"You want to take the nickel tour?"

Angie would have preferred to wait for her mother. Jim, however, seemed antsy to show her around.

"You probably won't sit still until I do."

"You're right. Come on."

Angie walked with him all around the property as he spoke of new windows, siding, shingles and a dozen other remodeling terms she'd heard him use time and again over the years. It was fun for her to watch his animated actions as he pointed to and then explained the different projects he'd either completed or was still working on. Angie would nod when he would turn to her, as if she completely understood the highly-detailed descriptions of his work.

Her Dad was the same as always. He had quick, rapid movements and a fast, sure way of speaking. The orderly way in which he spoke jogged Angie's memory back to her childhood feeling that all the thoughts and ideas of his craft were situated perfectly in his head. His medium-brown hair did seem somewhat grayer at the temples, but that was to be expected, he was nearly fifty-five. The word 'crisp' often came to her mind when she was in his presence. His clothing, whether work-type or casual, looked tailor fit to his trim build and his shiny cheeks always had the appearance of just having been shaved. Standing and talking with him, Angie didn't have to look up into his light-brown eyes. She and her father were the same height.

Finishing up the short tour, Angie followed alongside her Dad to a building near the lake's edge. What she assumed was a dilapidated boathouse, ended up to be his make-do woodshop. An old fashioned, cedar-strip canoe sat on padded sawhorses and took up the lion's share of open floor space. The canoe's entire inside, along with the top trim pieces had been reworked, sanded smooth, and were now heavily varnished in a honey-gold color. Fresh bronze rivets were implanted all along the outside length of the newly repaired upper edging and the underbelly had been painted a deep, hunter-green. Angie knew it must have taken weeks of painstakingly slow work for her father to refurbish the old craft.

The old-time warmth of the antique craft drew Angie close and she automatically ran her fingers along the glossy, wood-grained trim. She looked to her Dad, who was already smiling proudly.

"This is really something."

"Yeah, something to pass the time."

"No, Dad, this is beautiful enough to be on display somewhere. I wish I could have taken some 'before' pictures of this."

"It's not too late," Jim said, getting excited again. He waved for her to follow. "Here, look."

Right outside the door, Angie watched him peel back the heavy plastic cover off a similar, although yet to be repaired canoe. The difference between the two watercrafts was startling. The faded, worn-out wood of this canoe gave off the impression of being tired and weak, as if beyond any trustworthy usefulness. It was hard for Angie to imagine the gleaming canoe in the workshop had once looked this rough.

"Was the other canoe this rundown?" Angie wondered.

"About the same. But don't let appearances fool you. This old boy is just as sturdy as it was seventy years ago. It's seen a ton of use, but all it needs now is some tender loving care…and some caulking, for the leaks."

"How did you ever find these? Did they come with the cabin?"

"Nope. I made a deal with a guy down the road. He said I could have this one, if I fixed up the first one for him. Turns out these were the canoes his grandfather used in his guiding business, way back in the 1920's…you believe that?" Jim was grinning broadly. "Look, how wide it's built across the beam, for steadiness and carrying heavy loads. This design is outdated now, but I think it has way more character than the lightweight aluminum ones you see nowadays."

Jim patted the wooden structure, like he would an old friend.

"Nobody makes 'em like this anymore, Angie."

Jim pulled on the plastic cover a little more and pointed to some faint lettering at the rear of the weather-beaten canoe. It was barely visible, but she could read: P. Maki Guiding. Angie made the name connection immediately. It had to be a relative of the man she'd spoken with earlier.

"I think I met the guy you're talking about. The one who owns the resort down the road."

"You mean Ray Maki?"

Angie nodded yes.

"How'd you happen to meet…ah, you missed the turn-off."

"I was given poor directions."

Angie loved teasing him, a trait she had picked up from her mother.

Jim opened his mouth to defend himself and was cut off by the loud honk of a car horn. Angie turned and saw her mother waving excitedly from behind the steering wheel. She copied her Mom's wave and hurried to the car. Before they got close enough to hug, she took quick note of how good her mother looked. She had lost some weight and was dressed nearly the same as Angie, except for a green-suede blazer she wore over her own white blouse. Angie had always felt her mother's short and wavy, white hair made her look prettier, not older. After a lengthy embrace, Lois spoke to her daughter while still holding both of her hands.

"Once-a-week phone calls don't cut it, Angie. I'm going to have a serious talk with your father about all of his urgent projects that just can't seem to wait."

She shot an accusing look directly at Jim. He managed a puny smile and immediately tried to get off the hot seat.

"You two look like sisters."

"Nice try, Romeo. Do you really think an old canoe or new siding is more important than going to visit your only child?"

"It's more my fault, Mom." Angie purposely bailed her Dad out of trouble.

Lois was unwilling to put her daughter in the same tight corner where she had trapped her husband so she let Angie's remark pass. Instead, she fell back on a loving habit.

"I bet you're hungry. Too bad for you that it's Dad's turn to cook." Lois re-fastened her eyes on her husband. "Is supper ready?"

The question took Jim by complete surprise. Preparing supper had slipped his mind. He had no safe way to reply. The frightened look of a deer caught in the headlights of an oncoming car was comically stuck to his face. Angie and Lois burst out laughing.

"I was thinking that we could all go out to eat," Jim eventually said.

The excuse was lame and dreamt up on the spot. The two women laughed even harder. Lois took some pity on her husband and held out her hand.

"Come on, handsome." She planted a kiss on his cheek. "You've stumbled your way on to a good idea."

The three made their way to the house, Lois and Jim arm-in-arm. It pleased Angie to set her eyes on them. Once inside, she again saw the handprints of her father's work, all around. The main living space of the snug cabin also doubled as a dining area and a three-chaired table was pushed next to a new picture-window, where Angie had first seen her Dad's face. Placed all around on the fresh, oak paneling were paintings, photos and other familiar fixtures from their Duluth home. Fitted on either side of a stone fireplace was built-in shelving, backed with mirror glass. Her mother's eye-catching collection of old knick-knacks was evenly spaced between pictures of a youthful Angie. In one corner of the comfy, friendly-feeling room, a new curio cabinet hugged the walls tightly, a recent creation from her father's woodshop. It too, was filled with well-remembered bobbles and trinkets. Angie was reminded of their old home.

"You've been a busy boy," she said.

"Don't give him all the credit," Lois cut in. "I've done my share around here. Your father treats me like I'm a working member of his old crew."

"Very true," Jim agreed. "I've turned Mom into a class-A carpenter."

"Too bad I can't say the same about your cooking."

Angie laughed. She always enjoyed her parents' carefree digs at one another. She had heard it all of her life.

Rarely enough, Jim got in the last word.

"Hard work and my bad cooking. No need to thank me for your new girlish figure, dear."

If Lois had a response, she didn't bother. She was already on the phone making dinner reservations.

"Can you be ready to go in fifteen minutes, Angie?" Lois asked, covering the phone.

"Yes."

"We'll be there at six. Thanks, Ellie."

Angie got her purse and both women used the cramped bathroom to freshen up, taking quick turns in front of the mirror. Jim went outside to wait.

"Dad's right you know. You look great, ten years younger."

Lois smiled back at her daughter through the mirror.

"Something is bothering you. I can see it."

Lois knew her daughter very well. Well enough to know that Angie usually needed no prompting to say whatever was on her mind, except when it came to addressing issues concerning their small family. Then, often times her daughter would remain silent. Angie answered slowly.

"Well, you've told me before, its nice here and all that…but it's so far from everything. Are you sure you're happy living way out here?"

"Absolutely. We both are, Angie. It's like we're on a year-round vacation. And we've made friends with so many good people."

Lois finished at the mirror and tried reassuring a somber Angie.

"Other than you, moving here is the best thing your Dad and I have ever done together. He loves keeping busy and on the go. And we have no more business pressures to keep us up at night. That makes Dad happy, and me happy."

Angie had heard all this from their phone conversations. She already knew her Mom was doing well and always made good use of her own free time, volunteering two or three days a week at church. Lois had even convinced Jim into attending a majority of Sunday services. A fact that surprised Angie the first time her mother had told her about it. But Angie still felt perturbed, like an annoying rock was stuck somewhere inside her shoe. More needed to be said, but again, she decided to wait with her news.

Then Lois hit the mark.

"Are you happy we're out here?"

Angie wavered, then answered truthfully.

"It feels like we're drifting away from each other, and I don't want that to happen."

"Neither do I. The three of us had better talk. Later, okay?"

"Okay."

Angie barely got the word out of her mouth when they heard the repeated racing of a car engine. It was Jim's not-so-subtle way of informing them to hurry. Lois had recently broken him of his infuriating, horn-beeping habit and now Jim thought he had found a harmless way around it. Her Mom looked aggravated but decided it was best to let things slide, for now.

"Hyper Harry's got the jitters."

Angie had to laugh again. This was one of a dozen or so clever names that Lois had tagged onto her husband, and all of them fit him to a tee.

"We'd better get outside before your poor father blows the horn and finds himself inside a very deep hole."

Both women were able to get into the car before Jim caused any further difficulties for himself. They sat together in the backseat while Jim drove to the end of the long driveway. Angie was surprised when her father turned left, toward Lost Woman Resort.

# 5

Ray kenneled-up a tired Maggie and met his grandfather in the dining room of the lodge. Paavo was already seated at a table with two dear friends of the Maki family, Lee and Janine Church. The Churches lived directly across the road and would walk to the resort every Friday for supper, weather permitting. Other than his grandfather, Mr. Church was the man Ray respected the most, and held in highest regard - for good reason. Lee Church had fought side by side with Ray's father in World War Two.

From the Normandy invasion on, the two young paratroopers had formed an inseparable union, one that survived more than a few grisly campaigns. Their bond was so strong, that, in the fall of 1946, the Churches chose to move from their hometown of Chicago to live here in northern Minnesota. Thereafter, as their new lives and growing families intertwined, Lee and John's deep, mutual friendship had grown even stronger during their twenty six years together at Pike Point. When John Maki died in 1972, Lee Church retreated into a silent, private shell. A shell, some thought, where he partially remained.

After John's death, a young Ray had asked his grandfather; what was wrong with Mr. Church? Why was he so different now? And why hadn't he come to the funeral? Paavo had explained to his grandson that Mr. Church was full-up from all the dying he had seen, and there was no room left inside him for any more sad things. All Mr. Church needed was time, Paavo had said. Time to pack up the worst of his war memories, so he could empty them from his heart, and pass them on to Ray's father.

"That will be a big help to Mr. Church. Now your Dad can give all that trouble straight to God, and then He will get rid of it forever."

That made some sense to thirteen-year-old Ray because he had once come upon Mr. Church at the cemetery, head bowed and talking in low tones, as he leaned against John Maki's headstone.

Lee Church still looked every bit the warrior he actually was, even though he was nearly seventy years old. He always wore his hair 'high and tight', with a flat, military-style crown, and one side of his rough face was badly metal-pocked from hot shrapnel. Starting at his missing left earlobe, Mr. Church's neck carried a wide, ragged scar that slanted down and across, stopping near the point of his Adam's apple. The same artillery round that had seared and sliced open his throat had also separated Lee Church from the bottom half of his left leg. Ray had often wondered how it was possible for any man to have survived such mortal wounds. Mr. Church, Ray thought, had to be one tough customer.

Neither John Maki, nor Lee Church ever spoke of their time during the war so Ray had no idea how the two men had managed to live through the infinite brutality of that time. Growing up, Ray had a thousand questions that he always wanted to ask about the war but he never dared to approach the subject. Years later, when adult Ray returned home from his own military duty, Skinny had recited countless narratives about the battles and hardships endured by the soldiers of that era. Yet, even with Skinny's detailed accounts, Ray could only guess at how many times the threat of an unimaginable death had raged all around his father and Mr. Church. After John Maki died, Ray had resigned himself to the belief that he would never know anything about the personal wartime experiences of the two men.

There was, however, one irrefutable fact that Ray did know about the man. If an angry Mr. Church ever riveted his deep-brown eyes on anyone, you could be sure the other person would look away first.

Ray was certain, beyond all doubt, Lee Church feared nothing.

"Stupid thing," Mr. Church growled.

He used both hands to shift his artificial leg so a waiting Ray could sit next to him at the table. He slid his hated cane off the empty chair next to him and then handed it to Ray, so it could be hung on a nearby coat rack.

"I hope you don't mind sitting with us, Ray. Lee wanted some company."

"I don't mind at all, Mrs. Church," Ray answered politely. "It's not very often I get to have a meal with three of my favorite people."

Janine Church was the spokesperson for the couple, assisting her husband in conversation and sometimes finishing his short sentences. Mrs. Church did this because ordinary speech required much effort and air from her husband. The same searing metal that had pierced and burnt its way into his neck had also damaged his vocal cords. Lee Church spoke with the deepest voice Ray ever heard used by a human.

Mrs. Church was the polar opposite of her husband. She was shy, soft-spoken, and even tempered. Ray had known her all of his life and had never heard her raise her voice to anyone. She was by far, the gentlest person he'd ever met. The outdated glasses she always wore reminded everyone of a demure, though very likeable, school librarian.

Ray nodded at his grandfather, who seemed very pleased to be sitting with the well-thought-of couple. Paavo also had the utmost respect for the war-torn veteran and considered him a person of the highest character. He also thought the world of Janine Church.

"I order walleye dinner for us, Raymi."

"Perfect, Grampa. I'm in the mood for fish."

The four friends had a wonderfully slow dinner together, reminiscing about old times and re-telling familiar stories. And although it wasn't necessary, Ellie tended to their table closely, dropping in for a minute or two as she scurried about the buzz and hum of the crowded restaurant. She too, was extremely fond of best friends, Lee and Janine. For many years the Maki and Church families had all blended together into one boisterous and close-knit household. Ellie treasured their long-time friendship, always mindful of the help and comfort given to her after John's passing.

During her final visit to the group, Ellie stopped long enough to hear Paavo cap off the meal with an old story the other three at the table had never heard. She smiled and remembered as her father-in-law dusted off the long-forgotten tale. Only Paavo, she knew, could get away with telling this story in front of Lee Church.

Many years ago, Paavo started, toddler Kyla had raced to the ringing telephone that hung on the lodge wall. Like quicksilver, spirited Kyla was able to scramble up a stool and get to the phone before anyone else could pick up. "Lost Woman Resort," she had parroted into the handset. It was the rumble-voiced Mr. Church on the line, asking for John Maki. Paavo told of how Kyla's eyes had doubled in size as she handed the suddenly unwanted phone over to her father. She cupped a whisper into his ear, "For you, Daddy. It's a giant!"

The well-told story left Mr. Church wheezing, and trying to catch his breath. Before he was able to gain complete control, Kyla made a poorly-timed visit to the table to say hello. The sound of her voice sent Mr. Church into another long, low-throated spasm. Janine Church, on

*Pike Point*

the other hand, was much more sensitive than her husband. She reached for Kyla's hand and smiled up at her, as if she were in need of great sympathy.

Kyla left without saying a word, looking a bit confounded. She returned a short time later with a small, cloth-lined basket that was packed full with freshly-made, oatmeal cookies. They were her grandfather's favorite. She set them in front of Paavo and laid a hand on his forearm.

"You told me this morning that you would stick around a little longer if I made cookies. Well, Grampa, no kicking the bucket today, or tomorrow either...I made a double batch."

Paavo stared up at his granddaughter, deeply touched by her thoughtfulness. He knew how busy her days were, and how hard it must have been for Kyla to find the time. He looked over at Mrs. Church, who also seemed very moved. Paavo cleared his throat and coughed a little, trying very hard to reign in his feelings. Ray thought he might cry. The four people at the table looked to Paavo, hoping for his sake, that the old Finn still had the inner strength to find his voice.

He did.

"To have a good family like mine. How can one man be so lucky, Miss Janine?"

Surprisingly, Lee Church answered for his wife.

"We've known you for a long time, Paavo...believe me, luck has nothing to do with it."

It was the longest sentence Ray had heard him speak in many years.

The difficult moment quickly passed for Paavo and he ended up cheerfully sharing all of his cookies. Soon afterward, the Churches excused themselves to walk back home. Paavo, Ray noticed, lingered at the table. He could see that something was on his grandfather's mind.

"Jag tell me how Skinny gets hurt."

"I don't think anything's broke or busted, but he doesn't look too good, Grampa. Especially his eye." Ray confessed the rest. "He got pretty upset with me when I told him that I was going to force him to see a doctor."

Paavo stared at his grandson, not moving a muscle. Ray had seen this firm look many times in his youth and he knew exactly what it meant; Grampa was not very happy. Ray could almost see the old wheels turning in his grandfather's head.

"You can go for a walk with me? I always like to feel the Point under my feet."

"I'd like that, Grampa."

Ray followed his grandfather's slow lead as they ambled past the older cabins scattered along the rock-filled shore, east of the lodge area. Paavo would stop every so often and tell a short history by each little cottage; what year it was built, or why, because of the terrain, a cabin had to be built in a certain spot. He even pointed to specific trees that were planted in order to maintain privacy between buildings. Ray had heard all of this many times but he never grew tired of the telling.

And even though Paavo was three years into his nineties, he was still able to recite the long-past details of the hard work he and son John had done in the years they had shared together. His lengthy memory of Pike Point was fully intact. Paavo stopped again as he neared the last cabin. He waited for Ray to look him in the eyes.

"Sometimes, in the winter, before you are even born. I pull a sled and snowshoe out to check on Skinny…He likes that." Paavo added, "I bring him supplies…and respect. He needs them both, Raymi."

Ray understood.

Once Skinny allowed and accepted your friendship, it was then a matter of simple respect. If you gave it, you got it. Ray's concern for

Skinny's health was perfectly valid, but telling him that he would be forced from his home was not the right way to handle things.

And Paavo, in his customary, calm way had let Ray know that he had messed-up royally at Skinny's. Ray immediately agreed with his grandfather's judgment but took no offense from the soft-spoken rebuke. It had always been this way with Grampa and his dealings with the family; to point out any mistake in such a way as to offend no one, always careful of their feelings.

Ray thought, "Now comes the correction."

Paavo did not disappoint.

"Tomorrow, we have breakfast again, then we go see Skinny. If I say to him, 'Maybe you go to town.' I think he will listen. I can stay with his dog."

"Are you sure, Grampa? It's a really rough ride in that old Bronco of mine."

"If you keep all the tires on the ground, I be okay."

Ray remained apprehensive. It was a rugged trip out to Skinny's place and he'd have to drive very carefully with Grampa on board. Yet, Ray knew it was a workable plan and he recognized the good sense of his grandfather's idea. If Skinny paid attention to anyone, it would be Paavo. Just the sight of Grampa at his doorstep would set Skinny to thinking along friendlier lines. Ray knew there would be no unruly outbursts from the old hermit while in Paavo's presence. And now Jag wouldn't have to go. Ray felt a huge sense of relief and he made the acknowledgement.

"Thanks, Grampa. I really wasn't looking forward to wrestling Skinny out the door."

Paavo seemed not to hear. For him, the issue was settled.

"I like this extra ground we walk on, Raymi. Your Dad, he buys it after he comes home from the army…in 1946."

Ray finished the thought.

"It was bought with the money he sent home from the war. Money meant for you and Grandma."

Paavo nodded at the truth of his grandson's statements.

"My John, he pay a high price for that money. Only he should spend it."

Ray nodded at the truth of his grandfather's statements.

Paavo turned carefully in place and surveyed the area, his gaze finally settling on the long peninsula that meant so much to him. Ray closely watched the old man and wondered how many times his grandfather had done exactly that, in the last seventy years.

"Probably a hundred thousand times," Ray thought.

Paavo seemed to read his mind.

"A million times I look around me. And every time, I say, 'Thank You', in my head."

Paavo put a crooked hand on Ray's shoulder and looked at him hopefully.

"You know something, Raymi? I like to think if the richest man in the world wants to buy our Pike Point, that man will always be one dollar short."

"For sure, Grampa. As long as I'm alive."

Paavo re-started his slow walk.

"I was pretty sure I know that. But it feels good to hear you say the words."

The two continued on the well-worn path, to the last cabin. Ray knew what Paavo would say next when he lifted his walking stick and pointed to the small building.

"Miss Ellie Swanson. She stays here in 1957. My John and her fall in love…first look."

"Lucky thing for me and Kyla."

"Mr. Church, he hits the head on the nail. Some things not just luck. I always think John and Ellie be a gift to each other. Same thing when Mr. Church comes here to live. Those good things not dumb luck, Raymi. Sometimes, God send help. You know what I mean?"

"Yes. I do."

Ray had heard his grandfather make this reference before, several times. Paavo had said that his son was "too much alone in his head" right after the war. It was not until Lee Church came to live on Pike Point that Paavo had noticed dramatic changes take place in his very quiet son. And ten years later, when John was ready, 'Miss Ellie' finished up the healing Lee Church's arrival had started.

Paavo's logic was those two events were not accidents of fate. They were meant to happen. He claimed the Good Lord knew full well that Lee and John needed each other after the war. And then Miss Ellie, Paavo had said, refilled his son's empty heart.

Ray had no cause to doubt any of that reasoning. John Maki and Lee Church were closer than brothers. Also, his mother and father had always seemed very much in love.

"Ray!"

Jag was calling his name and hurrying toward them. He had a real nasty look on his face. When he got close enough, Jag pointed to the nearby rental, Cabin Eight.

"We gotta get rid of those dipsh…bozos."

Jag looked at Paavo and corrected the way he talked to Ray. He never cussed in front of Grampa Maki.

"What's wrong?"

"The family staying in Six told Kyla that they saw two guys out on the dock a little while ago, taking a whiz into the lake. There are women and kids all over the place, Ray. Those stupid morons gotta go."

"This ought to be fun," Ray thought.

He followed Jag down the path. Paavo was left to catch up.

Jag got to the cabin quickly and marched to the end of the short dock where the unfortunate pair sat in lawn chairs, drinking beer. Ray watched from a few feet away as Jag turned his baseball cap backwards and positioned himself behind them, leaning down, in between the seated men. Ray heard him ask if they had done the dirty deed.

"So what!" the bigger of the two men barked back.

"So this."

Jag already had a hand on the back of each chair. He gave a hard shove, emptying the chairs and dumping the yowling twosome into the icy-cold water. The back splash of their double fall caught Jag full-force and soaked him from the eyebrows down. He shot a wet, exasperated look at Ray, who could only shrug at his brother-in-law's bad luck.

"You rotten son-of-a-bitch," the heavy-set one snarled after finding his footing on the uneven bottom. He struggled to stay upright on the slippery rocks, chest-deep in the frigid lake.

"If either of one you dimwits says another word, I won't let you out until the sheriff gets here."

Jag spiked both chairs down onto the dock and wiped his face as best he could on a shirt sleeve. He waited a full ten seconds for a reply. Something about the threat had made the pair submit and they said nothing. The smaller man was already shivering hard from the cold dousing.

"And pick up your beer cans on the way out."

Ray saw his grandfather come out of the cabin, carrying a small plastic bag.

"I see this before, sometimes. Wacky-tabacky."

He handed the baggie to Ray, who was more than a little surprised to find out that Paavo would know of such things. Evidently, Grampa was more world-wise than he thought. Ray walked over to the dripping thugs who were now standing on shore. He stared into their eyes and recognized the dull-witted expression immediately. He'd seen that vacant look before, when he was an M.P.

"These guys are wasted."

He held up the dope to show Jag.

"Tell that snoopy old gimp to stay the hell out of our cabin."

The bigger fella glared and snapped his remark at Ray, but it was Paavo who made him pay for his lack of manners. Quick as a blink, Paavo brought up his walking stick and rapped the distracted man dead-center between the legs, doubling him up.

"Grampa!"

Ray grabbed onto the old man's arm. Paavo yanked free of the grip and ignored his grandson. He leaned forward, into his victim, waiting for the groaning to stop.

"Not *your* cabin, sonny-boy. *My* cabin," Paavo corrected. "And you talk nice to old people, or maybe next time, I knock a little harder."

Ray tried his best not to smile. The last thing he wanted was for the situation to get any more out of hand. It was already bad enough. Nevertheless, it was nice to see a fire could still be lit in the old man's belly. He purposely placed himself between Paavo and his opponent, to prevent further trouble - from either one.

"Let's take it inside," Jag suggested, looking at the people who had started to gather.

Paavo was more than satisfied with his contribution, so he set out for the lodge.

"I want them gone, Ray. Trouble is, Cheech and Chong here are too screwed up to drive."

Ray knew that Jag was trying to avoid the big commotion a phone call to law enforcement would create. It was bad for business.

"Your call," Ray told him.

Jag turned back to the wet, shaking louts.

"Let's see. Indecent exposure, a bagful of dope, and who knows what else."

Both men stared at Jag. He had gotten their attention.

"As far as I'm concerned, you pissheads have only two choices, so listen close. We can call the sheriffs' office right now, like I said…Or, you can stay inside the rest of the night, like good boys, and then leave quietly in the morning. Either way, your booze and your weed are gone… Choose."

The thin man spoke up quickly.

"We'll leave in the morning."

That wasn't good enough for Jag. He stepped forward and went nose-to-nose with the second man.

"You're pretty quiet, Orca. Let's hear your answer."

The man backed away from Jag and gritted out, "In the morning."

"Good…Now, for your own safety and good health, do not make us come back here tonight. If everything works out, you can pick up your beer when you leave tomorrow."

Jag turned to Ray.

"Hand me those boxes."

Ray handed over both cases of beer and then emptied half a quart of vodka into a small sink.

Ray and Jag left the cabin without another word. Halfway back to the lodge, Jag whispered, "That guy must have stepped on a big nerve. I've never seen your Grampa act like that."

"I noticed Orca crawled under your skin pretty quick. Apparently, the fatass has a knack for it."

"Everybody's gotta be good at something." After a pause, Jag added, "Next time, I'm gonna call the sheriff right away."

Ray answered him, using Paavo's accent.

"It be too late to squeeze, Jag. After the shit is in your pants."

"You're completely weird, Maki."

Both men soon caught up to Paavo, who was almost at the lodge. They stopped alongside.

"You got 'sisu', Grampa. Lots of it."

Ray looked to a smirking Jag who knew the word and its meaning. They wiped away their grins after seeing Grampa's angry face.

"That chickenshit say that it be his cabin," Paavo fumed. "Me and John build it. That's where your Mom and Dad fall in love. I hope each breath tonight that mouthy bastard will think of me."

"I do believe he will," Ray accidentally chuckled.

"Especially if he gets an itch," Jag laughed.

Paavo looked at the two comedians, trying hard not to smile with them.

"All you American-born kids," he tisked. "What a big headache you are."

Just then the Holters walked out of the lodge, escorted by Ellie. After noticing the three men, she waved at them to come over.

Ellie started introductions but stopped short when she saw Paavo blinking rapidly. His head was tipped back slightly and his mouth hung open. The old man took hard-hold of Ray's arm and seemed unaware of his surroundings. Ellie stopped a small squeal with one hand and then froze in place.

"I be in Heaven, Raymi?"

"No, Grampa," Ray answered evenly. "You're not in Heaven."

Paavo straightened himself up.

"But now I know what it will be like. There will be beautiful women… all around me."

Ellie let go of a relieved sigh. She gave a long, sideways look to Paavo and then smiled weakly at a snickering Lois and Angie.

"The wise guy is my father-in-law, Paavo Maki. Be careful girls, he's a very big flirt."

"I'm Jim Holter, Mr. Maki. Nice to finally meet you. This is my wife, Lois, and our daughter Angelica…Angie."

Paavo shook hands, intentionally saving Angie for last.

"Angelica." Paavo repeated the name lightly, with a gleam in his eye. "I told you I be close to Heaven, Raymi. She has the name like an angel."

He laughed with everyone else, at his lucky wit. Angie saw her chance to add to the fun and promptly turned to Jag.

"You're all wet, Myron…and thirsty."

Jag stared down at his damp clothes and the beer he carried. For once in his life he was stumped for something to say. Very casually, Ray slid his fingers into the jean pocket that held the confiscated baggie, making doubly sure any edges were tucked out of sight. He had forgotten to wash the contents down the sink drain and now he grew nervous. No good could come from her catching sight of something like that. He stood perfectly still when she leveled her big green eyes his way.

"Nice to see you again, Ray Maki."

Ray mumbled something incoherent. He suddenly felt guilty, like a little kid who's been caught stealing cookies. Fortunately for him, Paavo came to the rescue.

"Jag give swimming lessons today," Paavo said happily, elbowing Jag.

"This time of year?" Jim wondered, "The water's kind of cold for that, isn't it?"

"He gives those people what they are asking for."

Angie could tell by Paavo's sly smile and his wording, there was a lot more to the story. She shifted her attention from the befuddled Ray to the cute and obviously alert old man. Upbeat, elderly people like this were her favorites.

"Ray told me earlier, you're the one who built Lost Woman Resort, Mr. Maki. I have to tell you, it's beautiful here. And the lodge is perfect, inside and out."

"Thank you, Miss Angie. But I don't do everything. I always have lots of help." Still, Paavo loved the compliment. "I think I will be a happy man when you can say, 'Grampa Maki.'"

"I'll make a deal with you. I'll call you Grampa Maki, if you drop the 'Miss' and just call me Angie." She then held up a finger. "Plus, you must tell me how old you are."

Angie knew most older people this sharp and quick-witted were not embarrassed about their advanced age. In fact, they were usually quite proud. Ray and Ellie looked at each other and waited for Paavo's standard answer.

"I be ninety-three, Angie. I should be ninety-four, but I was sick for one year, back in Finland."

Angie's giggle burst forth instantly. It was the same one Ray had heard earlier and he liked hearing it again. Paavo seemed to enjoy it also. She took two quick steps forward and gave Paavo an unexpected hug.

"You are a devil, and a delight, Grampa Maki. I'm so glad to have met you."

"You see that, Raymi? Less than one minute and I get a hug."

"That's because you're irresistible," Ray admitted. "A real smoothie."

"I told you to be careful of his flirting, Angie."

"Too late, Ellie. I'm already under his spell."

The group continued mingling and talking, with Jag soon excusing himself so he could bring the beer to the kitchen cooler, and then change into dry clothes. Ray turned his back on the group for a minute and pretended to speak with Jag. He discreetly stuffed the baggie into Jag's shirt so he could finally be rid of it. The bag had been burning a hole in his pocket since meeting Angie again.

Jim Holter was excited and animated as he related to Ray and Paavo the details of his progress with the canoe project. He told the two men that he was well aware the old craft had a long history and he would be proud to present it back into their hands, especially now, after meeting the original owner.

"The only thing left to do is paint the lettering on the back," Jim said. "In a couple more days, it's all yours."

Paavo seemed very satisfied to hear the old canoe was restored to its former self and that it would be home again on Pike Point.

Ray too, was glad.

He was also distracted. Every so often, Ray would catch himself pulling away from the conversation as he glanced over in Angie's direction. She appeared not to notice him as she talked easily with Lois and Ellie. Ray also tried to catch sight of a ring on her left hand. He had never done that type of thing in his life and felt some happy, mixed-up guilt after finding out that Angie did not wear one.

What Ray didn't catch, however, was that Paavo hadn't missed a thing. He'd had a nice talk with Jim Holter right enough, but all the while he had also tuned into Ray's preoccupation with Angie. The old man was in high spirits after they all said their goodbyes. He was soon left alone with his grandson.

"You can take me home now?"

"It's time for me to call it a day, too."

They started across the road to where the Bronco was parked.

"That Angie, she be pretty enough for two girls. You think so, Raymi?"

"She's alright."

Paavo said nothing. After they got into the truck, he spoke again.

"Next week sometime, you take me to town."

"Sure, Grampa. What for?"

"For you, Raymi. I bring you to the eye doctor. We get you some glasses."

It was well past eight o'clock before Ray was able to settle on to the short sofa in his sunporch. Maggie sprawled out on an oval rug in front of him and Ray absent-mindedly rubbed her back with his stocking feet.

With heavy eyelids and an occasional head-bob, Ray watched the lake gradually drift from a deep-blue to a shimmering black under the soft light of a rising half-moon. Sometime later, a low whistling in the trees announced to anyone who cared to listen that a change of weather was on the way. Roused from his half-sleep, Ray watched as a disagreeable west wind intentionally brushed up against the easy-going swells on the lake. Predictably, a few thousand watery flashes rose up in resistance. Ray benefited from the age-old squabble between wind and water when the frantic waves flickered their shiny pieces of broken moonlight in his direction.

A fitting end to a disorderly day.

Indeed, this day had been like no other and a reawakened Ray rolled through the ups and downs - the good-humored breakfast with Paavo, the trouble at Skinny's and Jag's reluctant agreement to help, the fun and memory-filled supper with the Churches, and finally, the difficulty at Cabin Eight. Like watching his own private movie, Ray reeled the day's events through his mind's eye as he pulled each one from his head. Eventually, he got to the scene where they had grouped together with Angie and her parents.

When Ray thought of her, he unconsciously rubbed the heavy whisker-stubble on his cheek while taking notice of the day's stains on his frayed jeans. He pulled out at his shirt front and spotted the purple trail of a renegade blueberry that had escaped from the snack he'd eaten on the bumpy ride out to Skinny's. Ray shook his head from side to side and wondered what she must have thought. He had certainly not made a very good first impression.

Still, the pleasing image of Angie hugging Paavo showed up and stayed with him for a while. It was good of her to go out of her way and be nice to his grandfather. She was obviously a very considerate person. No small wonder she became a nurse.

Ray's back came off the sofa.

A nurse! He remembered Lois Holter showing off a photo of Angie and then telling him that she was some sort of special nurse…Maybe she could help Skinny. It was a lot to ask, seeing as how she'd just gotten here…But she did seem like a nice enough person, and a trip to Skinny's wouldn't take all that long. Anyway, what would hurt to ask? The worst that could happen is she'd just say no.

Definitely worth a try.

Ray almost got to his feet. He purposely stopped the momentum of his thoughts and decided to give the brainstorm more deliberation. That's what Grampa would do. No use creating another mess, like he'd done once already today, at Skinny's.

But the more Ray tossed around the idea, the better he liked it. There would be no jarring ride for Paavo, and hopefully, no big fuss out of Skinny. She'd probably be able to tell if the old crab actually needed a doctor. And even if he didn't, maybe she could do a little something for his eye, or put a real bandage on his arm. They could bring the big First Aid kit from the resort if she wanted.

In the end, Ray felt his plan was a good one. He decided to make the call.

# 6

ANGIE MADE A QUICK CALL home, and as expected, got the answering machine. It was a Friday night after all, so chances were good that Tina and Jessie would be out with friends. Angie worried about them when she wasn't there, although she took some comfort from the fact that both were good kids and had shown they could take care of themselves. She left a message for them to call back tomorrow. It would be reassuring to hear their voices.

In the bathroom, Angie washed her face and readied herself for the quiet evening ahead. She slipped into a well-used, dark-red night shirt and a lightweight pair of gray sweatpants. She put on her favorite pink footies and then curled up on a padded wicker chair in her parents' three-season porch. Jim closed the last of the windows against the cooling night air and then sat next to Lois on a matching wicker couch. He was not one to beat around the bush.

"Mom told me what you said. And you're absolutely right, we don't get together enough and I'll make sure that I..."

"There's more to it, Dad."

Angie told them of the offer for promotion and got the exact reaction she had imagined; warm hugs, happy congratulations and a couple dozen excited questions. As always, Jim went to the practical side of the matter.

"This sounds like a big deal, Angie. If you need any help, of any kind, even if it's just to mow your lawn, Mom and I will be there."

"It's been that way all my life, Dad. I want both of you to know that. I can't tell you how much that means to me. What it has always meant to me."

Angie saw her Mom and Dad squeeze hands. Lois scooted forward, so she could see past Jim.

"You should be doing cartwheels right now. There must be something else."

"I'm feeling very selfish about all this, Mom."

"Selfish? In what way?"

"Well, I sit here and feel bad about not seeing you guys enough, and if we're going to be honest, that's mostly my fault. I think I'll be making matters worse by taking the job." Angie looked away, toward the lake. "It's like my career takes precedents over everything, even you two. I was leaning toward accepting, but now I can see that it's very self-centered."

"I have never known you to be that way," Lois stated firmly. She took a long look at her daughter. "Seeing Dad and I more often is a weak reason for turning down an opportunity like that."

"There's more," Angie admitted. "I love the one-on-one contact with the patients. I'll lose that if I take the promotion."

"Well if you don't feel right about any of it, then why are you still considering?"

"It's hard to explain."

"Try me."

"Okay…Right now I'm able to diagnose and treat a wide range of issues. I can even prescribe some medications. But in a way, I'm also limited because I see only a small percentage of the total number of people who come in to the clinic. That would change, if I was Nursing Director."

Angie leaned forward, for emphasis.

"Anyone who walks through the doors of a clinic meets a nurse at some point. And I'd be the one who has the most influence as to the handling of *every* patient, and the quality of care our nursing staff gives out."

"If I understand correctly, what you want is for people to actually feel cared for."

"Absolutely, and I'm not the only one. Most everyone in medicine feels the same; Nurses, N.P.'s, Physicians." Angie carefully weighed her next statement. "It bothers me to no end when I see sick people being herded through the system like cattle."

"I didn't know it was like that at your clinic." Lois was somewhat surprised.

"That's an overstatement on my part," Angie acknowledged. "And don't get me wrong, our medical staff is top-notch. But we are also overwhelmed at times, and one of the primary reasons is money. I really shouldn't say too much, but as far as the clinic's business people are concerned, the more patients that I am able to treat in a day the better. There are times when their 'bottom line' feels more like an assembly line. One patient after another."

"And you think you can change all that?"

"Part of me wants to try. Look, I understand the clinic needs to make a profit, no question. I also understand that it doesn't cost a dime to be nice. To treat people as courteously and as professionally as possible, and not like they're just another inconvenience stacked up in an over-crowded waiting room...The way I see it, that would be my main challenge, to help strike a fair balance between profits and proper care. And I think I can get us closer to that balance. Maybe I'm being totally unrealistic, but that's the discussion I plan on having when I meet with the clinic's Board next week."

Lois smiled. She was very proud of the person her daughter had become.

"Nothing you've said sounds self-centered. As a matter of fact, the exact opposite is true. You sound caring and dedicated, not selfish."

"I like to think so Mom, but if the career choices I make have a negative impact on the three of us, then maybe I better choose differently. I refuse to put Dad and you on hold." Angie sat quietly for a moment, reflecting. "I talk big about creating a balance at the clinic, but I can't seem to create one in my own life."

"Your mother has spent thirty years trying to teach me priorities."

Jim had been silent up to now. He jumped into the discussion with both feet.

"I may have an answer to part of the problem. Or maybe I should say, a better way of doing things."

Both women looked his way. Jim started slowly.

"Okay. The way I see it, you will never be short of work, Angie. So finding the time to visit Mom and me on a regular basis will be tough. And now, with all the extra travel time, it's even a bigger pain. For us two, staying in hotels is a little inconvenient and kind of expensive when we make the trip. Am I right?"

Jim took their silence as his permission to continue. He held up both hands and went on carefully.

"This is only a suggestion, and I hope I'm not stepping on anyone's toes." Jim looked to both women before continuing. "What if we finished-off your basement? It's part rec-room already. Mom and I could put in a corner bedroom for us, and maybe a small bath. Like a separate area for us to stay. You know, to keep out of each other's way if we need to."

Angie warmed up to the idea immediately and a laundry list of positives popped into her head. She could keep her girls; they lived upstairs with her. And no more hotel bills for her parents, which meant they could stay longer. She could use their help around the house when her schedule got tighter, like she knew it would.

The telephone rang loudly in the other room and interrupted her thoughts. Lois got up to answer.

"It will increase the value of the house," Jim said confidently. "Well, what do you think?"

"Maybe you should sleep on it, Angie," Lois advised before leaving the room. "There is no need to decide in the next ten seconds...Hello."

Angie knew her Mom was right. She would need time to sort through these latest details.

"If we do this, Dad, I pay for the materials, no arguments, or handouts."

"Agreed. Mom and I will only supply the labor. Should take less than two week..."

"Telephone, Angie."

"Must be one of the girls."

Angie went into the next room and took the receiver Lois.

"What are you doing home on a Friday night?" Angie's bright smile disappeared. "Sorry, I thought you were someone else."

Lois left the room and took her place next to Jim, allowing Angie her privacy. Even so, they couldn't help but hear bits and pieces of the muted conversation.

"No bother, we're still up. What can I do for you?...Yes, I'm a Nurse Practitioner...What kind of favor?...Is this man a relative of yours?...And he lives way off in the woods. Let me stop you right there. I don't want to be rude and I'd like to help, but I don't even know you. You really can't expect me to traipse off into the middle of the woods with someone that

I know nothing about…I'm sorry too, but you're going to have to find another way to get help for your friend…That's perfectly alright, no need to apologize. Goodbye."

Angie came back into the porch. She stared at Jim and Lois.

"That's all I need. More things to think about."

"Some sort of trouble with the girls?" Jim asked.

"No. That was Ray Maki, of all people. He said some guy that he knows was injured a couple days ago. Something about his arm and his eye. He had the nerve to ask me to go with him on a house call tomorrow morning."

"Who got hurt?"

"I don't know, Dad. He never gave a name."

"I don't get it. Why the house call?" Lois wondered.

"Evidently, this man lives all alone, miles from anyone. He said the guy hardly ever sees anybody and refuses to come in to see a doctor. I mean, what sort of person lives like that in this day and age?"

"It's got to be Skinny Severson." Jim said, answering the riddle. "That's his work on top the curio."

Angie looked to the corner cabinet in the living room, at a scaled-down replica of a Mallard hen and her two ducklings. Lois had put a blue velvet cloth under the carvings and they appeared to be swimming their way along the top. One of the frowning hen's babies was halted in mid-flap of its tiny, immature wings.

"Do you know this Skinny guy, Dad?" Angie asked before plopping down into the chair.

"Only what I've heard. He's like a hermit or something. Anyway, he keeps to himself a lot. Ray has mentioned him before, when he was helping me with the rafter work, here in the porch."

"Well I'm sorry, but the whole story sounds pretty spooky to me. Doesn't it?" Angie looked from one parent to the other. "Besides, I'm not riding anywhere with someone I don't know. Especially into the middle of the woods."

Lois agreed whole-heartedly with Angie, yet she couldn't pass on the opportunity to harass her husband.

"Actually, it sounds very romantic. If it were me, I'd go. It's got to be way better than hanging around here with me and Woodchip Willy."

Angie knew the game was on.

"Maybe you're right, Mom."

"I can't believe you'd pass up the chance to be alone with a handsome bachelor like Ray."

"He is pretty cute. In a scrubby kind of way."

"You never know what exciting things might happen."

"I didn't think of it like that. Two single adults, all alone in the great outdoors, letting nature take its course. I'm going to call him back. Right now."

"Okay, I've heard enough." Jim stood up. "You know, Lois, for someone who spends so much time at church, you sure have a colorful way of thinking."

"I was just remembering the time when you and I…"

"Stop!"

Jim could take no more. He hurried to the other room and quickly closed the double French-doors that separated the rooms. He mumbled, "Gees, Louise."

"You'll have to tell me about it later, Mom."

Jim yelled through the glass panes, over the giggling.

"She'll do no such thing!"

Angie tossed and turned on the hide-a-bed in the living room. She kept glancing up at the shadowy ducks on top the cabinet. After midnight, she gave up trying to sleep and tiptoed outside. She was drawn down to the shore by the moonlight's wavering shine on the lake. Across the bay and to her right, she could see the orange firelight from a distant campsite at Lost Woman Resort.

There was much to think about, and so many questions ran through her head; what to do about her parents, the promotion, plus all the other clinic issues, and now a possible remodeling. The disquieting list cycled on an endless loop.

In time, a whiff of wood smoke nosed into her awareness and gently nudged Angie out of the lengthy trance, distracting her from important matters. A yard light blinked on behind her and she heard the porch door close softly. Her Dad stepped up and they stood shoulder-to-shoulder facing the lake.

"The wind died down. Now it feels like rain." Jim took off his jacket and draped it over Angie's shoulders. "You okay, Rose?"

"I'm fine, Daddy. A little restless. Still trying to unwind, I guess."

"I know the feeling well. It took me a long time to get used to the peace and quiet around here."

"Now that you say it, I don't remember hearing a boat all evening."

"You won't hear one. The north half of the lake is in the Boundary Waters, so there's no motors allowed on Lost Woman. Most of the lakes up here are like that. Makes for evenings that are almost too peaceful."

Angie was enjoying the small talk. It was a needed diversion.

"Lost Woman. Kind of a funny name for a lake."

"Ray Maki was telling me about that. He said the Chippewa used to run a con-game on the Voyageurs. After the French would make a big trade for an Indian woman, she'd up and disappear the first night out. Make it look like she had just strolled out into the lake and drowned herself, from unhappiness. Ray said that someone in the tribe would pick her up at night, then sneak her back home. She'd lay low for a while, in case the traders came back."

"Do you think it's true?"

"I don't know, that was two or three hundred years ago. Makes for a good story though."

Both became quiet, each waiting for the other to speak. During the silence, Angie made a quick decision. She was glad to settle one of her issues.

"I liked your idea about the basement. Let's go ahead with it, even if I don't take the job. When it's done, you and Mom are welcome to stay whenever you want, for as long as you like."

"Good. I know it'll work out, all the way around." Jim was done with the chit-chat. "You're the image of your mother, Angie. But I like to think there's some of me, in you."

"How so?"

"Well, I never enjoyed working under somebody else's rules. It always gave me a touch of heartburn to see a job done incorrectly. You know, cutting corners just to get the job done as fast as possible. I always hated sloppy work." Jim paused. "But once I was on my own, and playing by my rules, I could see what was good for my customers, was good for me. That's why I had to start my own business. Otherwise, I would never have been happy."

"I'm not unhappy at all."

"I know you're not. I guess I'm a little off point. What I'm getting at, is you are like me in some respects. You can see a better way of plying your craft. A way to improve yourself, and at the same time, improve the way medicine is practiced these days. What you said earlier about balancing healthcare and money is spot-on. I hope you trust your instincts."

Jim reached for her hand.

"Whichever way you decide, Angie, just do what's right for you. The good stuff you want for your patients will follow along."

"You're right, Dad."

Angie was quiet again. Jim could see her thoughts were still a ways away.

"What else you got?"

"I can't help but feel that I've been putting you and Mom on a back burner. Like the clinic and my career are more important."

"Get rid of that guilt. Your mother and I know that's simply not true. Both of us are well aware the career you've chosen has never been only about you. The facts are, you're darn good at what you do, so it comes as no surprise that promotions are part of the overall package. You've been a big help to a whole lot of people. Mom and I feel proud, not slighted."

"Thank you," Angie answered softly. "It's starting to sound like you want me to take the job."

"That's not my decision to make. The main reason I came out here was to make sure you don't let your feelings for Mom and me get in the way of that decision. It's your life Angie, not ours."

"I almost wish they would have offered the job to someone else."

"Well they didn't. Look, the head honchos at the clinic aren't your average, ordinary dummies. They're well-educated, so they realize with your schooling and your expertise, you are an excellent choice. They know you have a strong foundation to build on." Jim laughed lightly, at himself. "How's that for the start of another dumb carpenter analogy?"

"Mom always says you have a one-track mind."

"Focused, I like to think I'm focused about my work."

"I guess I have the same problem."

"And that's not such a bad thing, so long as you don't let it consume..." Jim stopped. "Well, I'm cold and I've probably said too much. You ready to come in?"

"In a minute."

Angie leaned into her forehead kiss and watched her Dad's silhouette walk briskly to the house. He called back to her when he reached the porch steps. The certainty in his voice carried easily in the night air.

"By the way, Rose. You're just as safe with Ray as you are with me. Maybe safer. He's good people."

"Thanks for the jacket."

Jim waved and disappeared into the house.

"And thanks for everything else," she whispered.

With a small smile, Angie wiped the rolling tear from her cheek.

### 7

"Dork," Ray said back to the mirror.

He swiped the last little patch of shaving lather from his face and rinsed his razor under the tap. He'd been restless all night and had awakened way too early, about four-thirty. Not able to sleep properly, he'd gotten up and used the extra time to tidy up the house, and himself. Outside, Maggie whined to come in from the cold and rain so Ray grabbed an old towel and met her at the back door. As he wiped her down, Maggie looked anxiously around for the earsplitting vacuum cleaner that had chased her out into the wet morning.

"Relax, will you? I put it away."

Maggie lay down cautiously under the table, ready to make a break for it, should the unfamiliar device reappeared and come screaming back to life.

Ray went to bedroom closet and switched into a new pair of pre-faded jeans. He pulled a light-grey tee shirt over his head and then he snapped together a dark-green, cotton-canvas shirt. He tucked in the tails and cinched up his belt tightly. He went to the laundry nook and pulled his wash-worn jean jacket from the hot dryer.

Ray was in a good mood, despite the awkwardness of the phone call last night. At first, he had been totally embarrassed. Later on, he'd gone to bed angry at himself for being so simple. He woke up realizing Angie was right, of course. They had probably spoken with each other a grand total of ten minutes. No sensible woman would do what he had asked.

"What a weenie," he said, slipping into the warm jacket.

Although he felt totally responsible for creating another clumsy mess, Ray still held on to a pocket of resentment because of Angie's blunt refusal. As dumb an idea as the phone call now seemed, it had also been an honest request, a request to help an old friend. Ray told himself, if she wanted blunt, that's exactly what she'd get from him. And no more going ga-ga over her good looks. The only drawback was he'd most likely not see her for a long while, maybe never.

"I can live with that," Ray said on the way out the door. "Come on, Maggie. Truck!"

After a faster than normal breakfast, Maggie huddled up inside her dry doghouse behind the lodge as Ray shut the kennel door. He was early to the resort and for the first time in years he had to unlock the back door. He turned on a few lights and lit the kitchen's grill so it would be pre-heated for his mother. Ray kindled some wood in the ancient, split-stone fireplace that occupied a corner of the lodge's dining room and then sat down to enjoy its crackling warmth.

As he waited for the rest of the family to gather, Ray looked up to the framed photos resting on the fireplace mantle. He scanned over all of them, his eyes eventually settling on his favorite. It was an old picture of his father and Lee Church standing tightly together in front of the lodge. Other than the fact both men were wearing their dress uniforms, there was nothing unusual about the photo. Also, neither man smiled when the picture was taken, but something about it always captured

Ray's attention, and admiration. That was due, in large part, to an old hermit.

Because of Ray's keen interest, and out of a great respect for John Maki, Skinny had related time and again the well-documented, World War Two accounts of the 82$^{nd}$ Airborne. The 'All-American Division' he had called it, given that young men from every state in the union had once served in its ranks. Many times, Skinny had recounted to Ray the four grueling weeks of fierce, hedgerow fighting that had followed the initial Normandy invasion, after the young soldiers had been told three days of hard combat was all that was expected from them. He had told Ray in great detail about the leadership mistakes of the British-led, Market-Garden campaign into Holland which had needlessly cost so many Allied lives. Skinny always spoke solemnly of the 82$^{nd}$'s heroic efforts during the freezing, inhuman conditions of the Battle of the Bulge, where Mr. Church had been so badly wounded.

That's why the old photo tugged at Ray so strongly, because when he stared at it, he saw first-rate men. Men who were an important part of his youth. Ray saw two lion-hearted soldiers whom he was extremely proud to have had in his life. Ray was looking at two authentic, American heroes.

He felt a light touch on his shoulder and heard his grandfather's old voice. Paavo gazed up at the same photo that absorbed Ray.

"In my head, I see your Dad's face, more and more."

"I'm not able to do that anymore, Grampa. He's been gone so long, it's getting harder for me to remember what he was like. I need the picture to remind me."

"Maybe I can see his face because I get closer to him, every day."

Ray turned away and stared back at the fire. He didn't want to consider it. Any serious thoughts he had about losing his grandfather were far too disturbing, and always instantly dismissed.

"I see my little Jenni and your Grandma. All the time." Paavo went on, "For a long time, I feel bad when I think of my Augusta and the baby. But now it makes me smile when my mind sees them."

Ray couldn't fathom how his grandfather enjoyed seeing the images of all the people who'd been taken from him; every one of them, before their time. Ray knew first hand the shocking circumstances of his Dad's death and it always saddened him to think of the missed years with his father. Paavo had also spoken of losing his baby daughter before her first birthday and of how his wife Augusta had passed away only one month before their son returned home from the war. What was good about any of that?

Nothing. Not a single thing.

"It feels too miserable when I think about it because they all died too soon. I don't get it, Grampa. They're all dead and gone, how are you able to smile about something like that?"

"I don't see them in a long time, Raymi. I be very happy when I can see them again, for real."

Ray wanted to bolt out the door. He remained seated, looking again to the fire.

Paavo asked quietly, "You can let me go? When the time comes?"

"There's no choice, Grampa. I'll have to."

"That's right. God choose that time, not Ray Maki." Paavo took Ray's upper arm in a steady, strong grip. "Something else makes me happy to see them."

"What?" Ray wished the whole uncomfortable conversation would end.

"When I see your Dad again, I can look straight into his eyes and tell him of his fine family. Then my son will say, 'You do good for them, Pop.' And he will thank me. That will be a nice thing to hear."

It was true. His grandfather had been a constant source of strength for the entire family for as far back as he could remember. Ray wanted very much to agree with what Paavo had just said but his response was trapped behind a hard-set jaw. The clear truth of Paavo's statement had struck Ray hard and he had to clench his teeth tightly to stop any emotion from spilling out. He loved the old man standing next to him like no one else.

"Anyone want coffee?" Ellie asked from behind them.

Both men nodded yes, so Ellie tipped two cups right side up on a nearby table and filled them near the top. She made her way over to Ray, bent down and kissed his cheek. Ray looked up at his mother and gave her his usual one-arm hug.

"I'm hungry, Ma."

Ellie smiled sweetly at the familiar line. She stared down at her son with dewy eyes and gently rubbed the light lipstick off his cheek. The tender look in her eyes caused Ray to wonder how much of the conversation she had heard.

"Breakfast will be ready in ten minutes. Let's fill you boys up before you go off to Skinny's."

The same caring look stayed on Ellie's face as she gave Paavo's hand a long, loving squeeze.

"You, Paavo Maki, deserve a world of thanks from John…and me."

Ellie had heard everything.

Kyla did a double take when she came down into the dining room, not expecting to see either Paavo or Ray. Jag followed close behind.

"Now there's a couple of things you hardly ever see," Kyla observed.

"You mean, seeing two good-looking Finlanders in one spot?" Jag winked at Paavo.

"No. Ray cleaned up, and on time."

"You do look very nice, Raymond." Jag finger-waved daintily, enjoying his own humor.

Paavo stepped on his fun.

"I think Jag change his mind about taking sauna with you, Raymi."

Kyla frowned at her husband. She quickly dismissed her grandfather's odd comment and smooched a morning kiss on his weathered cheek.

"Boy, two days in a row, Grampa. Those must have been pretty good cookies."

"Best I ever eat. But I should tell you, I only get one cookie. Your Jag, he comes to the table after you leave and eats up all the rest."

"No I didn't!" Jag looked scared. "Honest, Kyla, I didn't have any."

Kyla saw the sparkle in Paavo's eyes and decided to take up sides with him. It would be a lot more entertaining if they all ganged up on her husband.

"If you had half a minute's chance to eat every single one of them, you sure would have."

"Thanks a lot, Grampa Maki," Jag pouted. He sat down beside the grinning old man and waited for Kyla to enter the kitchen. "Now that you got her fired-up, she'll be in my face all day."

"I just try to even up the score, that's all."

"What score?"

"Ellie tell me that you show your boys how to catch the birds. Then they catch the trouble. But there is no trouble for Jag." Paavo returned the earlier wink. "By suppertime, my Kyla will make everything, even-steven."

"No doubt," Jag whimpered.

Ellie and Kyla shuttled back and forth from the kitchen as they brought out the meals and then joined the three men at the table. Kyla flaunted a small plate under Jag's nose and set it next to Paavo. On the plate were two oatmeal cookies. Ray knew that Grampa was right about

Kyla. She'd make Jag pay all day, even though it was for the wrong crime.

Ray swigged down a mouthful of black coffee and a tiny portion of joy when he remembered in mid-gulp that it was Saturday. They could all have an undisturbed breakfast together because Billy and J.P. were still in bed. There would be no morning turmoil. As soon as the happy thought passed, there was a knock at the door. Ellie was closest so she got up to answer.

"Tell whoever it is, we're not open yet," Kyla said gruffly. She echoed Ray's thoughts, "Just once, I like to have a quiet, uninterrupted breakfast."

"Good morning, Angie."

Everyone looked up, except Ray. He stared at the cinnamon on his oatmeal.

"Come on in. Have you eaten?"

"Yes I have, Ellie. Thank you."

"Coffee's on the table, if you'd like some."

"I would. Good morning, everybody."

Angie greeted them all and all answered back, except Ray. From the corner of his eye he noticed the black bag she carried. She set it by the coat rack, hung up her wet umbrella, along with a waist-length Mackinaw coat. Her oversized, maroon and gold, U of M hockey jersey drooped casually outside the dark-blue jeans she wore.

"Come and sit down, Angie," Paavo said. "Jag, you slide over so she can sit next to me. And don't spill food on her when you eat."

Kyla smiled at Angie, and her husband's continued verbal pounding. She filled a cup with fresh coffee and set it on the table, next to where Jag had been sitting.

"I'm Kyla Jagunich."

"Angie Holter. Nice to meet you. I believe I bumped into your sons, yesterday afternoon." Angie put a hand on Jag's shoulder. "It must be hard raising three boys so close to the same age."

"Two. We only have…"

Kyla caught the wisecrack in mid-sentence. She loved it. Everyone laughed, including a reluctant Ray and a surprised Jag.

"I apologize, Myron. I couldn't resist."

"That was a good one," he admitted. "And everybody calls me Jag."

"Okay, then I will too."

Angie sat down directly across from Ray.

"And I also owe you an apology. Usually I'm more polite than I was last night on the phone. If it's still alright with you, I'd be glad to try and help your friend."

"Thank you."

Ray's resentment toward Angie evaporated but it was immediately replaced by a surge of self-consciousness. No one else at the table knew of the evening telephone call and he suddenly felt a few pair of curious eyes on him. Ray felt his face grow warm and he silently cursed himself for blushing. In spite the embarrassment, he was not willing to let Angie accept any blame for the improper call. It was time to swallow some pride.

"I should never have called and put you on the spot like that. You had every right to say no. You know nothing about me."

"My Dad gave you a high recommendation. That's all I needed to know."

Angie had said the perfect thing for him to save face. Ray was smiling when he turned to Paavo.

"She's a specially-trained nurse, Grampa. Do you mind if she takes your place?"

Paavo did not answer right away. He seemed to be giving the simple matter an awful lot of consideration. After a time, he nodded repeatedly, as if agreeing with an unspoken conclusion he had reached in his head.

"Better for everyone if Angie goes with you. Tell Skinny that I say 'hello', and that he should listen to the enkeli that comes to help him."

"I will," Ray chuckled.

"What's enkeli?" Angie asked.

"Angel," Paavo answered. "Like your name."

The dark gray clouds seemed satisfied with their complete soaking of all things beneath so they hurried off, allowing the sky to lighten in their absence. All around, the resort was waking up to a typical May morning in northern Minnesota. Vacationers wearing sweatshirts or light jackets, and long pants, crowded their way into the lodge for an early meal before heading off for a full day of outdoor enjoyment. Some would stay here, on Lost Woman Lake. Most others would be crossing into the BWCA for a lengthier stay - to camp, fish or hike the trails that were deep inside the rustic confines of the park. Whatever the choice, by mid-afternoon the majority of them would be down to tee-shirts and shorts, along with a thin layer of bug spray.

Ray and Jag stood near the old Bronco and Angie waited in the passenger seat.

"We won't be gone too long, Jag. I'm thinking we should be back by ten."

"Take your time. Kyla woke up the boys and I'll put them to work as soon as they eat."

"Here's a leash. I forgot to ask Grampa to look after Maggie."

"Okay, okay, I'll take care of it. Just get in and go already."

Ray did as he was told and Jag shut the door for him.

"Alright, see you later, Jag. Good luck with the guests in Cabin Eight."

"I think I'll let Feast and Famine sleep it off for a while. Then I'll send your Grampa down there with his walking stick. That should rattle their little cages."

Jag beamed at his own joke and then leaned in the driver's side window. He spoke past Ray, to Angie.

"You're gonna have a ton of fun at Skinny's. I sure hope you got a straight-jacket in that black bag."

Angie's eyes opened very wide.

"Thanks a lot," Ray said flatly.

"You're welcome. Only trying to help out, Maki." Jag walked away tee-heeing.

"Straight-jacket?"

"Jag's getting back at you for the ribbing you gave him at breakfast. Anyway, he's always telling me that Skinny's a little spooky."

"Great. Don't I feel better."

Spooky. The same term she had used last night after the phone call. Angie felt a sharp ripple shoot up her back when Ray started the Bronco.

"Don't worry, Jag's dead wrong about Skinny. He's a terrific guy. Just a little high-strung…and unpredictable." Ray looked at Angie's worried face. "Do you have any tranquilizers for him, in case I'm wrong?"

"If I did, I'd probably take one right now."

The trail to Skinny's never looked better. Long, low-angled prisms of sunlight cut their way through the old-growth pines, creating a dramatic, double effect by spotlighting the dripping green of the wet forest while also casting areas of dense shadow. A steamy, ground-hugging mist was parted in half and shoved aside when Ray's truck rolled through its middle. Every so often, an irritated breeze would relieve the upper branches of their raindrops and a mini-downpour would find its way to the Bronco; a faint-hearted form of punishment for having unfairly dissected the harmless fog, and for disrupting the quiet of the backwoods.

Ray reached up near the sun visor and shut off the noisy wiper motor.

"I hope I'm not taking you away from something important."

"You're not."

"You keep looking at your watch."

"Sorry, bad habit."

"Well, I'm sorry for the rough road."

"I'm fine."

Angie squinted through the raindrops, at the tight trail that lay ahead.

"I'm surprised your grandfather would dare make the trip."

"I was a little worried about that. But he's a pretty tough old guy."

"Cute, too." Angie smiled now. "Why did he call me that name? Inka-something."

"Enkeli," Ray corrected. "Grampa called you that because he figures you're an angel."

"You can't be serious. He thinks I'm an angel?"

"Well, not a real one." Ray laughed at her cute expression. "It's because of your name. In his mind, it's not just a coincidence that a nurse showed up at the right time to help Skinny, and that her name happens to be Angelica. I know it sounds kind of silly, but Grampa has always had an old-fashioned way of looking at life. Probably a leftover, from the Old Country."

"I think it's sweet," Angie said. "He seems like quite a character."

*Pike Point*

"One in a million," Ray confirmed. He added, "I've noticed the older he gets now, the more he talks about heaven and angels, even his own dying. Things like that."

"I hear it all the time. Mostly from older people." Angie was beginning to relax, so she teased, "What about you? Do you think I'm an angel, or a coincidence?"

"Neither. I think you came to see your Mom and Dad. Skinny lucked out, that's all."

Angie turned and stared out the side window, looking at nothing in particular. The mention of Skinny's name had caused the uneasiness to come creeping back.

"Pretty, isn't it?" Ray prompted.

"It's beautiful. I wish I could enjoy it more."

With that said, Angie decided she'd had her fill of wondering and worrying about this unknown hermit.

"What's this Skinny Severson like?"

"Smart, very smart. That's the first thing that comes to mind. And he's big on respect."

"Has he always lived alone?"

"I think he's always been single but I can't say for sure. He's been around here long before I was born. Grampa and my Dad used to visit and bring supplies to him. Neither one ever said anything about him being married. Myself, I've never heard Skinny speak of any family. Or anything else about his personal life."

"Very private man, but I guess that's obvious. What else?"

"I can almost guarantee that he'll be a handful. I mean, he does have a temper, but he won't go crazy. Not the way Jag thinks he might."

Ray gave his answer more thought. He knew she wanted to know more.

"Skinny lives out here because he doesn't like people very much. He can barely put up with being around anyone. He says almost everybody he's ever met feels entitled to an easy life, and they don't appreciate why they have it so good. One of his favorite things to say is, 'The best generations are well behind us.'"

Angie nodded, soaking up the information.

"Sounds like a defense mechanism."

"What do you mean?"

"I'm sure there's much more to the story, but in very broad terms, people generally disappoint him. By living way out here, he's able to keep everyone at arm's length, to save himself the trouble of any more disappointment." Angie added, "You and your family seem to be the exceptions. Probably because all of you have respected his privacy."

"That sounds about right."

"I've met patients like that. For whatever reasons, they keep to themselves as much as possible and seem to dislike the few people they do meet. That kind of behavior allows them to be in control, and keeps people at arm's length. From my own experience, you have to prove yourself likeable, or capable, before those types of people will even give you half a chance."

"I've never thought about it that way. I think you're right because I brought Jag out here one time and that's exactly how Skinny treated him. I felt bad because the old guy never said a word to Jag. He acted mad the whole time, and all he did was shoot dirty looks Jag's way. Like you said, Skinny never gave him half a chance."

"Let's hope I have more success than Jag."

Ray was impressed. She had pegged the old grump pretty good.

"Tell me more, Ray. Whatever you can think of. The more information I have the better. I don't want to walk into a hornet's nest with only this bag in my hand."

"Skinny has always reminded me of an old scholar. He's got tons of books. Biographies, autobiographies, history books, all true-life stuff." Ray kept on, not knowing exactly what she needed to hear. "He carves and paints for a living, mainly birds. And he's meticulous about it."

"A realist...with high standards." Angie spoke the words quietly, mostly to herself.

"I don't know if it matters at all, but he has a little dog."

"A pet? I'm surprised."

"Skinny swears up and down she's not a pet. He told me that her job is to keep mice and other vermin away from the house and garden. He says that's the function of her breed, but I honestly think he enjoys having the dog around."

"He even has to make up an excuse to hide his soft spots."

Ray saved the worst for last.

"He will probably be drunk." Ray raised his eyebrows and put on a sheepish grin. "You know, to help himself get through the pain of the last few days."

"Perfect. He's stubborn, too."

Just before they entered Skinny's little house Ray and Angie swapped moods. She was calm and confident, he became tense and unsure. Ray knew that Skinny could be a ruthless buzz-saw when in a rotten frame of mind and he was now very worried Angie was overmatched. He hoped it was early enough in the day for the old coot to still be sober.

He was half right.

Ray went in first and turned on the lights. The supply boxes were in the same spot where he had left them and Skinny sat in his usual spot, the high-backed chair that faced away from the door. Ray tried his best to start off on a friendly note.

"Grampa says 'hello.'"

Skinny ignored the greeting and went on the offensive.

"Two doors banged shut on your truck. I certainly hope, for your own benefit, you had the foresight to cart along your tractor-ass brother-in-law. Circumstances in the very near future may call for your desperate need of his assistance."

Ray's heart sank to his stomach. Angie saw the anxiety on his face and took over.

"He brought me."

Ray saw the old man's thin arm give a sizeable flinch. A woman's voice was completely unexpected. Still, he did not turn their way.

Bridget took a long leap off the bunk and yapped her way over to sniff Angie's ankles. Once satisfied, she went back to her guard post on the small bed.

"Ahh, Ray," Skinny moaned. "What in the name of God's Green Earth are you doing?"

Ray said not a word and quickly grabbed the crate from under the washstand, setting it alongside the hefty workbench. When he looked to Skinny, he was again shocked. If anything, the old guy looked worse than yesterday. His injuries seemed unchanged but the old man's face was very pale and tiny beads of sweat dotted his entire brow. And now Skinny's good eye was blood-shot, from the drinking and lack of sleep. His white, three-day beard had the effect of making him look even more haggard and gaunt. He sat in the same slumped pose and wore the same sleeveless undershirt from the day before. Ray doubted if Skinny had even gone to the trouble of feeding himself.

Angie set her bag on top the worktable, careful of the half-full whiskey glass and unfinished loon carving. She handed her coat to Ray and sat down on the edge of the crate. She studied the blinking, surly-faced man and waited patiently for him to speak first.

"I will assume you are a physician."

"No. I'm an N.P., a Nur…"

"I don't recall ever hearing that particular term - N.P. The initials must stand for Nosey Person."

"Nurse Practitioner."

"Perhaps you should leave and practice on someone else."

Skinny appeared highly pleased with himself. He reached for a sip of whiskey, as a reward.

"Ray asked me to come here, to see if I could help his friend. He's very concerned."

Skinny grunted a loud 'humph' at an on-looking Ray. Half a second later, to Ray's horror, he leaned forward and blew a wet raspberry straight at Angie. She jerked backward, froze in place, and then turned a red, furious face toward Ray.

"I forgot to tell you about those," Ray said timidly. "Sorry."

Angie kept her eyes fastened on Ray as she slowly and steadily turned her head back to Skinny. She closed her eyes, took in a deep breath and made a huge effort to pull back on her anger. After getting a tight hold on her temper, she addressed the smirking, self-satisfied old man.

"That, was extremely rude, Mr. Severson. And in this day and age, that sort of behavior is also considered dangerous. *Never*, do that again."

Her glare penetrated right through Skinny and her voice vibrated with anger. Ray closed his eyes because the old man appeared ready to spray another one in her direction. He waited for the final blow that would put a quick end to this whole debacle.

It never came.

When Ray re-opened his eyes, he saw Skinny taking another drink as the old man leered back at him, over the rim of the glass. He recognized the same dirty look given to Jag. While Ray squirmed in place, Angie started over.

"Over here, Mr. Severson."

Skinny turned and pinned the angry look onto Angie. She matched it.

"I can very easily walk out that door and never come back. No skin off my rear-end. But then, that won't ease the pain in your eye. Will it?"

Angie waited and received no response.

"From everything I've been told, Ray's entire family has always cared about you and your well-being. They're all hoping I can help you, and frankly, I do not want to disappoint them. And I certainly don't want a ninety-three year old man racking his bones on a needless ride out here to check on your welfare, just because you're too damn stubborn for your own good."

Her last sentence was the perfect thing to say. The look on Skinny's face changed instantly, from one of disdain, to one of realization. The statement about Paavo had cut deep. When Ray saw the change take place he wanted to pump his fist in the air and jump for joy. Angie had the old man by the short hairs and Ray knew it. Damn…she was good at this…very good.

Skinny spoke after an unsuccessful, blinking staredown.

"What is your name?"

"Angelica Holter. And yours?"

"Roger Severson."

His first name was news to Ray.

"What is your plan, Angelica?"

"To do a quick examination." Quickly, she added, "In order for me to perform that properly I will need to ask you a few questions along the way. And that's not because I'm a nosey person. It's standard procedure."

Skinny nodded, "You have my permission to proceed, up to a point. I will let you know at once if you happen to cross a line I don't want crossed."

"Agreed. How and when did these injuries happen?"

"I was struck by a falling treetop, three days ago."

Angie seemed skeptical so a nervous Ray cut in.

"It really happens sometimes. To woodcutters."

"Did you lose consciousness at any point? If so, for how long?"

"Yes, immediately, for a matter of seconds."

"Have you had any headaches, nausea or vomiting?"

Skinny slowly tipped his head to the side and pointed to the whiskey glass on the workbench.

"I will take for granted the effects of an alcohol-related binge and the ensuing hangovers are not relevant. The answer to your three-part question is no, no and no."

Angie took the black bag off the table, opened it wide and set it next to her on the floor. First, she checked his pulse.

"How old are you, Roger?"

"Sixty-four."

Ray would have guessed ten years over.

"How old are you, Angelica?"

"Twenty-eight. Your pulse is steady and strong, although the rate is slower than normal. Possibly the result of the medication you've been drinking."

Next, she wrapped a blood pressure cuff around Skinny's left arm and readied her stethoscope. He pointed to the jersey she wore.

"Have you attended the University of Minnesota?"

"Yes. No more talking." Once finished, she handed the cuff over to Ray. "Your blood pressure is a touch low but nearly ideal. One-eighteen over seventy-two."

"Possibly the result of the medication I've been drinking."

Skinny was happy to have returned the serve. Angie ignored the remark and pulled a penlight from the bag.

"I'm going to examine both of your eyes. The light may be uncomfortable but try your best to do as I ask."

Skinny nodded his assent. Angie looked to Ray.

"Would you please turn his chair directly toward me?"

Ray jumped at the chance to help and did as she asked. He pivoted the chair on one leg and set it down carefully. It was at that point when he noticed the butt of a very large revolver sticking out from a homemade pocket sewn onto the right-hand side of the chair. Ray was instantly reminded of Jag's bazooka comment. He decided to keep quiet about the pistol, no point in alarming Angie. Ray convinced himself that the handgun was probably always there, he had just never been on this side of the chair. Still, he stayed where he was. Just in case.

Angie examined Skinny's eyes as thoroughly as was possible, given the conditions. She said nothing, clicked off the penlight and put it back in the bag. The tiniest of grins darted across her face when she pulled another plastic case from the bag. Knowing both men were watching closely, she suddenly frowned at the label.

"Oh no."

"What?" Skinny and Ray asked at the same time.

"I packed the wrong thermometer. Would you mind standing up? This is a rectal..."

"If you think, for one single second, I am going to tolerate that sort of...!"

Skinny's blazing-mad statement was snuffed out by Angie's endearing giggle. After seeing the old man's stunned, angry expression, she let go completely. She kept laughing, harder and harder, as she looked from one dumbfounded man to the other. Angie made an honest effort to apologize, although she didn't have much success. Skinny tried to restrain himself, though in short time, he too, was pulled into the moment. Ray stood still, open-mouthed, completely amazed by the whole surprising scene. He had never heard Skinny laugh out loud.

"Where in the world did you get her from?" Skinny asked after things quieted down.

"You told me to never end a sentence with a preposition."

Skinny jerked around, looking angry again. Ray tensed and glanced down at the pistol. The old man noticed, then smiled.

"No need for worry, Ray. I surrender, without a shot."

"It's about time, Skinny."

"Put this under your tongue and keep your mouth closed," Angie snickered.

Skinny held up a hand in protest, uncertain of the thermometer's previous whereabouts. A sick look spread out on his face.

"I, ah...I am not so sure."

"Here." Angie swizzled the working-end of the thermometer in the whiskey glass and then stuck it in his mouth. "Think of it as an eighty-proof lollipop."

Angie snapped on a pair of disposable gloves and gently unwrapped the dishtowel from Skinny's arm. The entire area was covered in heavy ointment and smeared blood. As she carefully cleansed Skinny's upper arm, angry-looking cuts as well as fresh blood began to appear. The jagged injury was worse than Ray had imagined. With a roll of gauze, Angie encircled two large sterile bandages around his arm and then removed her gloves. At her request, Skinny handed over the thermometer. She read it, wiped it down thoroughly and put it back in its case. Angie turned back to her patient, all business again.

"You did an excellent job cleaning the wound. I could find no debris whatsoever."

Skinny gave Ray an I-told-you-so look.

"However, your arm needed considerable stitching, but it's too late now. Left as is, I consider it an open wound and prone to infection. That may be why you are carrying a low-grade fever."

"What is your opinion of the eye?"

"Taking into account the alcohol consumption, movement and reaction in both eyes is within normal parameters. Judging by your obvious discomfort and the nature of the injury, it's highly likely the cornea of your right eye has been scratched, although I cannot confirm that diagnosis. Not here. I would need a special dye and a black light. It's a simple, painless procedure. As is the treatment."

"Left untreated, will the eye heal on its' own?"

"Possibly. Although it's definitely not worth the risk, or the on-going pain. It's an injury you really can't afford to ignore." Angie pointed to the carving on the bench. "Not if you want to continue doing the beautiful work you do."

Angie then saw she had slipped past Skinny's defenses when a soft sadness emerged on his face. Despite all of the outward bluster, inside, this was a deeply-sensitive man. She reached out and placed her hand on top of his.

"Look, Roger, I don't have the right to tell you what to do. That will be your decision. What I *can* tell you, is that you will feel significantly better within minutes of treatment. And if you choose, I will stay with you the entire time."

Skinny stared at the unpainted loon clamped to the workbench. He silently stroked his moustache while he made his decision. Ray held his breath.

"Thank you, Angelica. What you have said to me makes perfect sense. And I accept your kind offer of an escort." Skinny turned to Ray. "However, today is Saturday. Is it not?"

"Someone will be at the clinic," Ray said, closing the loophole. "And Bridget can stay with me and Maggie while you're there."

"Will the clinic accept a cash payment?"

Ray shrugged, so Angie answered.

"They will bill you."

"Use the resort's address, Skinny."

"One last thing, Roger. I would need to follow up within twenty-four hours of your initial treatment. If you could possibly make yourself more available, I would appreciate it. I'm on vacation visiting my parents and…"

"Say no more. I am sure our friend Mr. Maki can put up with the inconvenience of Bridget and me staying at his home for one night."

"No problem, Skinny," Ray said, smiling broadly. "I'll do whatever it takes to get you fixed up."

Ray sat on his folded jean-jacket that he had placed atop Skinny's laid-down crate. The thin jacket offered little padding, although it was better than nothing. Angie bumped her way over another half-exposed boulder and Ray was nearly launched to the far corner of the truck box. He hung on with both hands for all he was worth and cursed the two-seated Bronco.

"Sorry about that!" Angie called out the partially opened window.

"I'm good."

Ray looked into the truck and saw Skinny and Bridget smiling back at him. Both dog and man seemed to be enjoying his suffering. Right then, the next in a long series of suddenly released raindrops fell from the high branches and pelted down on his head and shoulders. Skinny awarded him a cheerful thumbs-up from inside the comfort of the half-cab.

"Are you sure you don't want my umbrella!?"

"How the hell would I hold on to it?" Ray muttered.

"What's that?"

"I'm good."

Ray was good. Or most parts of him were, anyway. He dared a quick wave at Skinny and flashed a fake smile back at him. But Ray really didn't mind his predicament. He felt his mild discomfort was small potatoes when compared to the misery his old friend must have endured over the past few days.

Actually, Ray was somewhat shocked the sticky situation had worked out this well. Who would have ever guessed a total stranger could get the old crab to go the clinic, let alone talking him into spending the night away from his home? Angie had accomplished the near impossible in his opinion. She had cracked a very tough nut…so to speak.

Angie jerked to a sudden stop next to her car in the resort parking lot and a half-soaked Ray gladly hopped out of the box. She watched him in the rear-view mirror as he shook out his flattened jacket and then unsnapped out of his wet shirt. She had given a lot of thought to all the trouble he'd gone through to help Skinny. Few people would have gone to that much bother. Now Angie regretted being so direct with him on the phone. She also hoped that she hadn't hurt his feelings last night, or embarrassed him in any way. He had only wanted to help a friend. She got out and met Ray at the rear of the Bronco.

"Sorry, Ray."

"For what?"

"For the trip back, I mean." Angie kept the rest of the thoughts to herself. "I think I gave you a rough ride. Are you alright?"

"A little wet but I'm good," Ray said cheerfully. "Thanks-a-million for doing all this. I know it was a lot to ask."

"You were completely in the right to ask for my help. Roger's condition may have only deteriorated." Angie could see the instant relief on Ray's face. "Would you phone my parents? Tell them I'll try to make it home by noon."

"Sure, I'll call the minute you leave."

Skinny slowly made his way to the back of the truck and stopped next to Ray. He handed over a worried Bridget, a small bag of dog treats, and a second bag containing a change of clothes. Carefully, he stretched his back.

"You may want to consider updating vehicles, Mr. Maki. This model is well past its prime."

"This was Dad's truck," Ray said a little too seriously. "And besides, it's not even twenty-five years old. Barely broken-in."

"The only thing broken-in, may be my tailbone," Skinny countered.

"I think it was my driving, Roger."

"Untrue, Angelica." Skinny scrambled after realizing his slip. "You did quite well, given the difficult conditions."

"Does that also apply to her, back at your house?"

"It does," Skinny admitted. He pointed to the small bag, trying to create a diversion. "Bridget's favorites are the brown, liver-flavored ones."

"I'll keep a close watch on her. Promise."

For the second time in less than a day, Ray watched Angie's taillights disappear from view. A fidgety Bridget whined under his arm so Ray bent closer to her perked up ear.

"Don't worry, girl. The old grouch is in good hands."

Ray paused, and then whispered again, to the empty roadway this time.

"She never gave the man half a chance."

# 8

Ray had just closed the kennel door after treating Maggie and Bridget to an early noon snack when he heard an engine roar to life. He knew right away who it was; the troublemakers from Cabin Eight. Ray thought nothing of the noise, just two idiots blowing off some steam. They would be gone shortly. But a few seconds later, when he heard the pickup blast out from the parking lot, Ray found himself in a long, uphill sprint to get to the front of the lodge while hoping for dear life that no kids were in danger. He tried to spot Billy and J.P. as he ran but he couldn't see them so his head filled with sickening pictures of his shattered nephews.

Ray was already seething by the time he heard his grandfather yell. "Leeee!"

He turned toward the voice coming from the front porch. Just barely, whipping past the branches of the trees, he saw the speeding truck closing in on Mr. Church. Ray put himself into a higher gear, knowing in his heart that he would be too late. Mr. Church was going to die a horrible, bloody death and there wasn't a thing he could do.

The whole scene was so bizarre, so out of place. This was all wrong, and so unfair. Ray's mind reeled and sent instant, awful thoughts through his head. And the helpless feeling made him sick to his stomach. The exact same feeling he'd had when told that his father was dead.

At that precise moment, Ray no longer felt anything like himself. The red-hot fury that burned in his gut disappeared, replaced at once, by a numbing, cold-blooded rage.

The Ray Maki he knew, had left him.


Facing the sudden end of his life was nothing new for Lee Church. This time, like all the other times death came for him, he turned toward it, completely unafraid and ready for a fight. And this time it would not be a long-range artillery blast that got him, like in Belgium. No, this fight would be close-quarters. At least now he could stare into the eyes of the men who wanted him dead. He raised to his shoulder the only weapon he had at his disposal, his cane. As the enemy truck came at him, Lee Church took aim and thought of his best buddy sitting on the lodge bench; the one who had hollered his name, and who would now witness his dying. He hoped John wouldn't take it too hard. He thought too, of his girlfriend Janine, back in the States.

But Mr. Church was confused. No one wanted him dead anymore. And it wasn't his best friend John sitting on the bench. It was Paavo. A heartbeat later, Lee Church realized that his mind had flashed back to an earlier, uglier time in his life. He understood his mistake. It was the desperate call of his name that had sent him crashing back to December, 1944.

Mr. Church's mind cleared quickly as he remembered everything. All he had wanted to do was bring the resort's mail over to Paavo. Somehow, he had gotten caught up in the middle of some sort of prank, a very sick and stupid one. Still, he stood his ground and waited to see if he would be run over, his cane clenched tightly in his hands.

Time to settle up. The big man sat in his truck sneering at his good luck and his wicked idea. There, up ahead and a little more than fifty yards away, was his slow-moving target. This was his chance to scare the holy hell out of the old man who had taken a cane and cracked him square. The nosey one from last night. The one who had embarrassed him in front of a bunch of people. He revved the motor several times, jammed the truck into gear, and took aim. He gritted his teeth as the rear tires spit out wet gravel onto the other cars in the parking lot. He cackled with his buddy when they saw the crotchety old man was paralyzed in place.

This was going to be sweet.

At the last possible second he stood on his brakes and stopped the bumper of his pickup only inches away from his victim. He leaned on the horn and laughed some more.

But the old man never moved a muscle. And he didn't jump at the blasting of the horn. As a matter of fact, he didn't seem frightened at all. The old crip just stared straight at him, pointing his cane like a rifle, and looking like he was ready to kill.

Dammit!

The big guest from Cabin Eight had a smoked-up, drunken memory of the evening before so he didn't know the wrong person was in front of him. Even with the man standing only a few feet away he still didn't realize his mistake. He put his truck into reverse so he could back up and go around the crazy, snarling feeb. Then he and his friend could finally get the hell out of here.

That's when things started to go bad.

As events unfolded in front of him, Ray slowed to a walk and an overall calm settled in. His breathing slowed and he zeroed-in on the small world directly in front of him. Like never before in his life, he felt relaxed, and ready, in touch with every tingling fiber in his body.

Ray nodded when the truck ground to a stop...good. He grinned when he heard Mr. Church swear at the driver...even better. Ray chuckled to himself when he saw the much-hated cane snap in half as it came down onto the hood of the truck.

"No big deal," Ray thought. "I'll ask Skinny to make him a new one. Diamond Willow this time."

Ray was only a few feet away when Mr. Church toppled over into a dirty puddle on the wet ground, tripped-up from the overhead blow he had landed. The lower half of his artificial leg was twisted weirdly out of place and the metal brace of the knee joint had ripped through his pant leg. Mail was scattered everywhere. Ray took in the sad scene as he stopped next to the proud man who was struggling so hard to rise back up. He stared at the foolish pair in the truck. They would pay dearly for the indignity this courageous man now suffered.

Ray squatted down and pulled Mr. Church upright.

"Let me take care of this for you," he said quietly.

An out of breath Mr. Church could only grunt. Ray ducked under the old soldier's muddied arm and started to help him home. When they were clear of the truck, Ray spoke to the driver.

"Stay in the truck, Chubby."

Ray wanted the exact opposite but there was little reaction from the big man. He took two more slow steps with Mr. Church and then spoke out loudly, so all those who had gathered around could hear.

"I mean it, Marshmallow. You better keep your fat ass behind the wheel and waddle it home to Mommy. Before you get hurt."

That did it. He heard angry arguing coming from the truck. By the time Ray propped Mr. Church up against the mailboxes near the road's edge, he heard the truck's door squeak open behind him...good.

"He's coming Ray," Mr. Church rasped.

"I know."

"Go kick his goat-smellin' ass."

"I'll get 'em both."

Ray turned to meet the big brute who was lumbering toward him. He knew this type well. He'd seen scumbags like this in the army. This man coming at him was nothing more than a schoolyard bully, too afraid to take on others his own size, like last night with Jag, yet more than willing to face down anyone smaller than himself.

"Even better," Ray thought.

"I'm gonna beat the livin' shit outta you!" the truck's driver promised.

The big man was totally embarrassed at what Ray had said in front of the small crowd. And he was very mad about the deep crease in the truck's hood. Trouble was, he was too mad. He was so intent on the idea of pounding the smaller man into a bloody pulp that he made the simple mistake of telegraphing his first move. When Ray saw the man's eyes squeeze together, he automatically rose up on the balls of his feet and some M.P. training re-entered his head - most people were right-handed. Ray saw the beefy fist tighten just before the man swung.

Ray sidestepped easily to his left and let the white knuckles skim past his nose. He shifted his body weight back to his right leg and leaned into his punch, purposely hitting the off-balance man high on the neck, behind the right ear. It was an educated blow that was meant to stun and it did the job. He heard the man woof out, and then watched him stagger. Ray closed in quickly and waited for the man to straighten up. With textbook timing, he battered the man with another left hand, same spot. Ray watched him stilt around on rubbery legs and go down to all fours.

The fight was over.

"Not yet," Ray stated coldly. "Get up, tough guy."

He waited for the dazed man to get to his feet. When he did, Ray hit him with a head-snapping right hand to the mouth. The man crumpled backward, into an awkward-looking heap.

"Weird," Ray thought.

The exact moment he had delivered the punch he could have sworn the man had yelled his name. And of all things, the guy had used Ellie's voice. Then, from directly behind, the second man touched his back.

"Enough."

Ray's left foot instinctively planted and he spun around in a blur. As he twisted, his upper arm came up, away from his side. It was a reflex move, one he had done a thousand times during his training. The back of his elbow caught his sneak attacker on the end of the nose and Ray felt it give way. He watched the man sprawl to the ground, out cold and bleeding.

"Now it's enough."

"Ray!!"

There it was again, his mother's voice.

This time the scream reached Ray and he gave another look to the second man on the ground. This was no sneak attacker. This guy had only wanted to put a stop to the beating. As the adrenalin rapidly drained from his system, Ray started to shake badly. He gradually became aware of his family standing at the front of the lodge. He was forced to look up at them when he heard his grandfather speak strongly. Paavo was trying to get through to him.

"Raymi! Talk to me!"

Ray didn't quite have the full compliment of his normal wits so he misunderstood his grandfather's intent.

"I'd like to talk, Grampa, only I can't right now. I have to bring Mr. Church home."

"...Okay, you do that."

Ellie hurried to her son and clutched his quivering arm with both hands. Ray saw the pained expression on her face and he had to turn away.

"Come into the kitchen, Ray. Jag can walk Lee home."

"I'm alright, Ma," he tried to assure her. "I'll be back before you know it. Have Jag call the sheriff."

With his own mention of Jag, Ray glanced up to the porch once more and picked his brother-in-law out of the small crowd. Billy and J.P. leaned against their father, one on each side. The fearful look in the boys' eyes made Ray cringe. Kyla stepped down from the porch but he immediately turned away and started back for Mr. Church. It was then he noticed Angie's car parked a short distance down the road. She and Skinny were back from the clinic. They had gotten out and now stood behind the open doors of her car. Ray could think of nothing worth saying so he ignored them also.

At the mailbox stand, he again bent under Mr. Church's arm and bore most of the weight across his shoulders. From behind, he heard Angie rush over to the smaller of the two men on the ground.

"I sure messed up her whole morning," Ray whispered.

"Who's morning?"

"Grampa's angel."

Despite Ray's best efforts, Mr. Church labored hard, all the way to the house. The unwieldy exertion required extra air from the old soldier and he had to pull and push with long, low breaths. Their heads were close together, so with every grating exhale that came from the winded man, Ray was continually reminded of the deep, throaty clicks of an edgy jungle cat. When the two men reached the house Ray put an arm around

Mr. Church's waist and lifted, basically carrying him up the three steps of the front porch.

"Over there," Mr. Church rumbled, pointing to one of the twin rocking chairs.

Mrs. Church appeared at the wooden screen door and opened it halfway.

"Lunch is...are you okay, Lee?"

"I'm fine, Janine. Thank you."

"But your leg. And you're all muddy. Did you take spill?"

"I'm fine, mother." Mr. Church sat down heavily and then spoke politely to his wife. "If you wouldn't mind, Janine. I need to speak with Ray."

Mrs. Church said nothing more. She let the door close softly. Ray could still see her faint outline through the screen. She did not walk away.

"I should get going, Mr. Church. Ma looked pretty upset."

"It's important."

"Sure."

Ray sat down on the porch landing, his feet on the bottom step. He rested his elbows on his knees and stared at the remains of the tiny trembles in his interlaced fingers. Mr. Church rocked silently, looking out into somewhere. He stopped his chair suddenly and then stuck his fingers into the hole of his torn pant leg, ripping it down to the cuff. He hooked the toe of his twisted limb under the lower porch rail and leaned back. After a long, difficult pull, the leg worked loose and thumped down in front of the rocker, straps still buckled. Mr. Church stepped on the ankle of his loose leg and with a quick yank, the pant cuff was torn free. He bent forward, grabbed the edge of the hollow top and flung the whole works as far as he could into the front yard. It flipped to an upside-down stop, and tipped over, black shoe and white sock still intact. Ray stared at it, struck by the oddness of the sight.

"Stupid thing," Mr. Church mumbled in his window-rattling voice.

The old fighter shifted around in the rocker for a long time, trying hard to collect himself. Ray glanced over several times, waiting for him to begin; impatient to get back to the resort, unaware of the importance of what was coming. He did not understand that Mr. Church needed time. Time to dig down and find his way to some long-buried thoughts.

Eventually, Mr. Church found a starting point.

"Your Grampa sure got me snortin' when he yelled my name. He sounded like Hick…That's the name I gave your Dad in boot camp." Mr. Church repeated the name fondly. "Hick."

"I don't know why, but we hit it off right away…A hard-ass kid from Chicago and a hick from the sticks."

Ray nodded. From the corner of his eye, he could see Mr. Church's shredded pant leg swaying back and forth as he rocked. Ray also noticed that Mr. Church needed big gulps of air if he wanted to push out anything other than a short sentence.

"He was always goin' on about this place…Pike Point this, Pike Point that, all the time. And always talking about his Mom and his Pop…He was like an innocent kid. You know?"

"But that damn kid did everything right in training. Seemed kinda easy for him…I still felt bad for him because I didn't think he'd last ten minutes once the real shit hit the fan. I thought maybe it would be too much for a good guy like him…I was wrong, Ray. Your old man fooled me…He fooled everybody. It didn't take very long to figure out if you ever needed someone to back you up, or to watch your flank, you'd best pick John Maki…It was an honor to serve with him."

"You don't have to do this, Mr. Church."

"Oh yes I do," Mr. Church strongly disagreed. "It's the right thing to do, Ray. You got cheated out of a lot of time with your Dad and I want you to know the kind of man he was…The man I knew. This is something that should've been done, long ago…I guess this is as good a time as any."

Ray had to wait a couple of minutes for Mr. Church to begin again, so he didn't dare interrupt anymore. He wanted to hear everything the man had to say.

"There were a hundred and forty-six men in our original Company, including officers. Eleven of us made it back home…Eight of the eleven, in one piece. Your Dad was one of the eight."

Ray watched closely when Mr. Church shut his eyes and paused, preparing himself to speak about the unspeakable. His breathing deepened and the muscles in his jaw flexed time after time. When Lee Church opened his eyes he locked a black, lethal stare directly onto Ray. The absolute intensity of the look raised the hair on Ray's arms and he could physically feel the pure force of the unflinching will that ran through the old man in the rocker. Lee Church stared at him with the hardened eyes of a man who had witnessed hell on earth. Eyes that had never blinked.

"We were sent back to the front line because the Germans had busted their way back into Belgium…They had to be stopped, Ray. And that's exactly what we did. We were outnumbered and outgunned, but we stopped 'em…Dead in their tracks."

"Our company was told to hold our position, no matter what came at us. About mid-morning, they hit us a second time, real hard…Tanks and infantry. The next thing I know I'm laying there in the snow, bleedin' out. Didn't feel a thing…I remember thinking that I was so stupid, for getting hit…But I was happy, too. The insanity was finally over. No more killing, no more watching your buddies get shot to bloody hell, or blown to little bits…My number was up, Ray, and I knew it…I was so grateful about it that I laid there and thanked God Almighty for putting a painless end to all the misery."

Ray heard Mrs. Church sobbing softly from her side of the screen door. Mr. Church didn't seem to notice, he just sat perfectly still in his rocker, half a world away. His eyes were no longer focused on Ray. They were seeing far off into the distance, and almost fifty years into the past, completely wrapped up in the memory. He told the rest of his story the only way he could. He re-lived every gut-wrenching moment.

"Then here comes Hick. 'Leeee!!…You okay?! Oh, damn it Lee, they blew you up'…ahh God, the look on Hick's face…He starts screaming for a medic. I tried to tell him I don't want one."

Mr. Church touched the scar on his neck.

"I can't get out a word, so I'm thinkin', 'Please, leave me alone…go back to your foxhole and let me die in peace.'…I kept trying to push his hands away and then he says, 'You're not gonna die on me, Church! Don't you die on me!…I can take you home with me.'"

"The whole damn world is blowin' up and goin' to hell, and there's Hick, taking off my belt, wrapping it around my leg…Holding his hand on my neck…saving my life."

Mr. Church lowered his head and restarted his one-legged rocking. He pulled in another long breath. It took the old soldier some time to stuff the memory back into its far-off place. Once done, he stared at Ray again, but with a much softer look this time, and the start of a smile.

"And now here I sit…Wonderful wife, retired from the post office, got a nice home where Janine and I raised five good kids…Thirteen beautiful grandchildren who love their Grandma and their Grandpa."

"I ended up with a damn good life, Ray…I tell you all this, so you know. I'd have nothing, *none* of this, if it wasn't for your Dad."

Ray let the tears roll down his face. He made no attempt to hide or wipe them away. So many times he'd wondered about his Dad and Mr. Church fighting in the war, and what terrible experiences the two men must have gone through. So many questions he'd never dared to ask, either man. And how many times had he wondered how Mr. Church managed to survive his wounds.

Finally, Ray knew.

Ray leaned his head from side to side and used the sleeves of his tee shirt to dry his face. He lifted his head when Mr. Church cleared his throat. There was more to say.

"I'm sixty-nine years old. All things considered, that's a fairly long life. And in all that time, I have only one regret, Ray…Just one."

"What?"

"That I didn't go to your Dad's funeral."

Mr. Church's eyes welled-up for the first time.

"There's no need to explain anything."

"Well, that's the thing. I can't explain it to you…How close you get to a man in combat, the man who saved your life…Or how angry you get at the unfairness of what happened to him, and his family…How it tears you apart to see his life end the way it did, after all he'd been through…I can't put any of those feelings into words, Ray. I can only tell you, when your Dad died, it left me in a million pieces…I wasn't fit to be out in public."

"Nobody in our family has ever held that against you, Mr. Church. Everybody knew how you felt about Dad. And we've all seen you out at the cemetery."

"There is no excuse, Ray."

"My Grampa, he's pretty smart about these things. When I asked him why you weren't at the funeral, he told me that you were all filled up to the top. There was no room left inside you for any more dying."

Mr. Church looked away, bobbing his head, and slowly chewing his way through what Ray had told him.

"I guess he was right."

"Grampa has always told me that Dad got his life back when you and Mrs. Church moved here. He said Dad was too quiet when he got home from the war, and you were the one who saved his son, after the war was over."

A single tear rolled down Mr. Church's cheek. He used the palm of one hand to quickly swipe it away.

"I never knew Paavo felt that way. That means a lot, coming from your grandfather. He's quite a man."

"He sure is. So are you, Mr. Church. So was my Dad." Ray met the old soldier's gaze. "It's an honor to have known the three of you."

There was a long silence. Mrs. Church interrupted the quiet at the right time and she spoke softly through the screen.

"Lee, lunch is ready. You're more than welcome to join us, Ray."

Janine Church's gentle voice was a soothing bridge that her husband had used many times to get back to the here and now. He never failed to smile after crossing over. Ray too, felt the calming comfort of her voice.

"Thank you, dear. If you wouldn't mind getting my crutches please…I seem to be down to one leg again."

"Okay. I'll be right back."

Ray hung his head after hearing the proud man humbly ask for crutches.

"I better get going, Mr. Church."

Lee Church read Ray's face like an old book.

"I know what you Maki men are like, so don't you dare feel bad for me and my poor leg…It took your Dad a long time to get over that and I don't want to see the same look on your face…I'm not a cripple, Ray. You understand?"

"It's just that I better go back and see what kind of mess I got myself into."

"You did nothing wrong, so don't go hanging your head about that either...I'll tell you what, Ray. There are some sorry excuses for what pass as people in this world...And sometimes, they come knocking at your door, just begging for a kick in the ass or a thump on the head. All you did was oblige them."

Ray stood up and re-climbed the porch steps. He went to the rocker and held out his hand. Lee Church took his in a tight grip.

"I'd do it all over again," Ray vowed. "Thank you, Mr. Church, for telling me all this. I know it wasn't an easy thing."

"Turns out it needed to be done, for the both of us." Before Mr. Church let go of Ray's hand he said, "I need to ask a big favor of you."

"Anything."

"Could you fetch my sock and my shoe? Leave the leg for the woodpeckers."

By the time Ray reached the end of the Church's driveway he felt the full impact of what had taken place. For too many years, the images and memories of his father had been trapped in time. Whenever Ray remembered John Maki, it was through the eyes and mind of a thirteen year-old boy; a devoted son who had struggled very hard not to leave his father behind. But as time had passed, Ray was barely able to hang onto those ever-distant memories. They were old, faded remembrances now; ones that forever led to a sad ending.

That was no longer the case. Ray had been given a gift, a gift only Lee Church could give. At long last, Ray had a fresh, clear-cut image of his father; one that he could now look upon with the eyes of a full grown man.

John Maki, his father, had held up to the highest standard that was used to measure a man. A man who had done everything asked of him, and more, even through the worst possible circumstances. The fact that brave, wonderful men like Lee Church considered his Dad a special man among them filled Ray with an intense pride.

Ray Maki, the man, now held in his possession the long-awaited, everlasting link back to his father. No amount of time could erase the priceless imprint Lee Church had etched in Ray's heart.

Ray turned, but failed to catch sight of Mr. Church through the trees that filled the front yard.

"What an incredible man."

For nearly fifty years, every time Lee Church walked a step or spoke a word, he was reminded of the cruelty of war. And yet, without a trace of bitterness, he had said that his life was a good life. Ray was awestruck by what massive strength of character a man must possess in order to make such an unselfish statement.

Ray also realized how impossibly difficult it must have been for Mr. Church to speak of the hellish morning he and John Maki had shared out on the battlefield. He was sure it was an ugly memory that Mr. Church had intended to take to his grave, never meaning to tell a soul. But the old warrior had shared it with him.

"Thank you, Mr. Church."

"...Who are you talking to?"

Ray snickered at the sound of Jag's worried voice behind him.

"I was talking to Mr. Church."

"He's not even here, Ray. Are you alright?"

"Yup."

"You sure?"

Ray faced his brother-in-law.

"Never better, Jag."

"Well thank God for that. For a second there, I thought I was gonna have to throw a net over you."

"Where is everybody?" Ray wondered as he crossed the road.

The area in front of the lodge was nearly empty. There was no crowd, no truck, no commotion whatsoever.

"The Bruise Brothers couldn't get outta here fast enough. I think they were worried that Sugar Ray was coming back for Round Two."

"I can't believe you just said that." He shook his head. "Pretty corny stuff, Jag. You might be losing your touch."

"Only trying to lighten things up."

Jag stopped.

"Seriously, Ray. I didn't have time to call the sheriff. When Angie tried to help those fatheads, they told her to bug-off and got back in their truck. I figured good riddance."

"How about the boys?"

"They're good. Kyla already talked to them. When she was all done they went and asked her if she thought Uncle Ray would teach them how to fight."

"Ah, damn. I suppose I'll get an earful from her later."

"Better you than me," Jagged said. He whispered, "Don't tell Kyla that I said it, but I think she's proud of what you did."

"She'll probably still give me some hell."

"You can count on it."

Ray asked, "After I see Ma and Grampa, do you care if I get out of here for a while?"

"No problem, do what you gotta do. The boys and me have everything under control."

Jag grabbed Ray's arm as he started to walk away.

"Before you go." Jag hesitated, "I made those guys go back and clean up their mess in the cabin, otherwise they would've been long gone. All I did was get them worked up again and Mr. Church is the one who paid for it. This whole thing is my fault."

"It's okay, Jag." Ray patted his brother-in-law's big back, "You'll never know how much Mr. Church and I owe you for doing what you did. Thank you."

"You mean it?"

"Honest. Things couldn't have worked out better."

Jag grinned broadly, unsure of what he had accomplished but content to leave well-enough alone. He gave Ray a big, one-handed shove as he walked away.

"You know me, Maki. Only trying to help out." Over his shoulder he hollered, "Dizzy and Daffy. That's names I should've used."

Ray wanted to avoid the busy restaurant so he made his way around the outside of the lodge. Ellie spotted him from inside and hurried through the kitchen. She met him at the back door, unable to hide the concern on her face.

"Don't look so worried, Ma. Everything's okay. I'm sorry to upset you like that."

Ellie held her son close and did her best to hold back the tears.

"I thought maybe you couldn't stop yourself."

"I know."

Ellie forced herself to let go of Ray and then dabbed at her nose with the balled-up tissue in her hand.

"How is Lee?"

"He's doing great. Probably having some lunch about now."

Ray suddenly realized he was starving.

"I'm hungry, Ma!" he called out softly.

Ellie held her son close again, and cried into his chest.

# 9

"Would you like another peanut butter and jelly sandwich, Grampa Maki?"

"No thank you."

Angie knitted her brow. Paavo had been too quiet on the short trip from the resort to Ray's cabin. And all through lunch he had barely said a word. He hadn't eaten much, either.

"I'd offer you something different, only there wasn't much in the refrigerator."

"You do too much already."

"I'll have another, if you wouldn't mind, Angelica."

"Coming right up."

Angie hustled back to the kitchen and slapped together a third sandwich for Skinny. She was tempted to make one for herself but passed on the idea, saving her appetite for the better meal that most likely waited for her at home. She set the paper plate down on the table and looked around.

"Where's Grampa Maki?"

"He excused himself and walked outside."

Skinny had his appetite back. He gave a one-eyed ogle to the tasty sandwich Angie had placed in front of him and then refilled his glass with cold, chocolate milk. Many years had passed since the last time he'd eaten such a delightful meal. Bridget and Maggie watched his movements closely from the other side of the room, hoping more crusts of bread would be thrown their way.

"I've really got to get going, Roger. My parents are expecting me."

"Yes, of course." Skinny lowered the sandwich. "You were absolutely correct, Angelica. I do feel significantly better. I am hard pressed to thank you enough for all you've done on my behalf."

"I was glad to help," Angie said sincerely. "I'll see you tomorrow morning, about nine. Get plenty of rest and leave the eye bandage in place."

"I will do as you say." Skinny held up his hand, "One last item, if I may?"

"Yes?"

"I would ask that you not judge Ray too harshly. There is much more to the situation than you can possibly know."

"It's not my place to judge anyone. I'll see you tomorrow."

In fact, Angie had made a judgment. She just wasn't in the mood for any discussion. She only wanted to go home. Angie had witnessed most of the incident and found it all very disturbing, for everyone involved. To her way of thinking there was no excuse for the sadistic scene that had taken place in front of the lodge. And there was no good reason for the beating. None of it had to happen. It was all so stupid.

She scooped up her purse off the kitchen counter and hurried out the back door to finally head home. When she touched the handle of the car door, she stopped. She looked at her wristwatch and then dropped the purse through the open window. Angie couldn't make herself leave, not yet.

On the lake side of the house she found Paavo sitting on a double-bench swing. He was staring out over the lake as she sat down across from him.

"Is there anything I can do for you, before I leave?"

Paavo seemed not to hear. His quietness was cause for concern. After a few anxious moments on Angie's part, he finally turned her way.

"I meet you for one minute and I can see that you have a big heart."

Paavo looked at her so warmly, Angie was tempted to hug him again. She wanted to take him home with her.

"Your mother and father have a beautiful child. That must make them happy," Paavo tapped his fingers on his chest. "Inside."

"Thank you. That's such a nice thing to say."

"Thank you, Angie. For your help to our Skinny."

"You're very welcome."

Angie started to rise but she sat back down when she saw Paavo's distant look return. She was instantly annoyed at Ray for causing the distress she saw on the old man's face.

"Are you upset about what happened? The fight, I mean."

"No."

"That's surprising, because it bothered me."

"You think bad about Raymi now, but never in my life do I see him put a hand to anyone…Never. But this be different for my grandson, because today he fights for the best man on this Earth." Paavo looked at Angie, his voice higher and thickened with emotion. "Those foolish men, Angie. Raymi can not stand it when they shame Mr. Church too much."

Paavo pulled out a handkerchief from his back pocket and wiped at his face.

"Mr. Church, was that the man Ray helped to his feet?"

Paavo stared down at the swing's floor.

"Yes, Lee Church."

"Is he a good friend of yours?"

"He was my son John's best friend. Until my son died. They end up like brothers when they go through the big war together. Raymi always think of Mr. Church like a hero."

Paavo's eyes returned squarely onto Angie.

"You tell me, what kind of man would my grandson be if he cannot stand up for Mr. Church?"

Good question. What kind of man was he? The kind who obviously cared for the people close to him, or the kind who could mercilessly beat on those who angered him? Angie had seen two, very distinct sides of the man.

But Paavo, in his sincere and simply-worded way, had filled in some of the missing blanks. Little by little, during their short talk, Angie found herself softening her opinion of what she had witnessed. She looked at the gentle man sitting across from her and gradually came to understand Ray's powerful reaction much better. That was why Skinny had asked her not to rush to judgment. Both of these men, and her father, held a high opinion of Ray. All three could not be wrong. Angie also considered her own protective feelings she had for her Mom and Dad. That final thought toppled over her stiff viewpoint of Ray and the fight. She answered Paavo's heartfelt question.

"You're right, Grampa Maki. There are some people in this world worth fighting for."

Paavo said nothing. He was quiet again, and Angie couldn't help feeling some concern for his health. She knew it was possible for elderly people to be thrown way off by strong emotions.

"I don't mean to pry, but you do seem out of sorts. Are you feeling okay?"

"No, no. Nothing like that." Paavo searched for the right words. "It takes me a little while, but I think I figure it out."

"What did you figure out?"

"I think it is me that makes all this trouble for Raymi."

"You think that whole mess back there was your fault? How so?"

"Last night, those men, they be more than drunk. When the big one gets too smart with me, I hit him with this." Paavo thumped his walking stick on the swing floor. "Today, he sees an old man with a cane. He drives fast at him, because he thinks of me. He wants to scare *me*, Angie, not Mr. Church...Do you understand?"

"Yes, I do," Angie nodded. "I understand that some hung-over numbskull wanted to get even by scaring the daylights out of a ninety-three year old man. It's pretty hard to imagine anyone that ignorant."

"That be a good word for both of those men, Angie. Ignorant."

"I hardly think you can blame yourself for what they did to Mr. Church."

"But I make a big mistake last night, when I get into the middle. Now it is my fault that nothing goes the right way for my grandson."

"You lost me. What do you mean, 'nothing goes the right way?'"

Paavo didn't have to provide an answer because they both heard the sound of Ray's Bronco grinding its way toward them.

"There is my Raymi."

Angie helped Paavo off the wobbly swing floor and they met Ray in the short driveway. From the back of the Bronco, Ray grabbed several plastic bags filled with groceries.

"You be gone for a long time."

"Mr. Church wanted to talk," Ray explained briefly. "Ma told me you and Skinny were here, so I grabbed a few things from the kitchen cooler. I thought Skinny might be pretty hungry and I don't have much food in the house."

"Angie feed us a nice lunch." Paavo patted her arm. "Mr. Church okay?"

"Really good, except the knee joint of his leg came apart. You know him," Ray grinned. "He got mad and threw it into the front yard. Sock and shoe included."

"My God, he has an artificial limb?" Angie was stunned.

"He lost the real leg in World War Two." Ray handed a single bag to Paavo. "Could you go put this in the freezer, Grampa? I'll only be a minute."

"Ice cream," Paavo said happily on the way to the house. "Skinny not taste ice cream in a long time. That is a nice thing to do."

Ray waited for Paavo to close the door. He noticed that Angie had an especially sweet look on her face, as if she were pleased with something.

"How's Skinny doing?"

"Much improved. He ate three peanut butter and jelly sandwiches."

"I really didn't mean for you to do all that. I feel bad taking up your whole morning."

"Your Mom asked if I would bring Roger over here, your grandfather wanted to come with." Angie added, "And lunch really wasn't much of a bother."

"Well, I promise not to pester you anymore. Thanks again, for everything."

"I really should thank you. I can't remember the last time I've had such an unforgettable morning."

"Me, either."

"I am a little worried about your grandfather. He's upset. He thinks the fight was his fault."

"Jag tried to take the blame, too. Don't worry about Grampa. I'll talk with him later." Ray took a step toward the house and then stopped. "I sure hope you don't think I have that sort of trouble all the time."

"I've never seen anything so incredibly dumb in my life. And I have to tell you, I was highly upset with you and those men. I thought the whole thing was completely senseless."

With the thought of Angie and Skinny witnessing him out of control and brawling in the middle of the road, Ray blushed brightly.

"I'd do it all again," Ray said with conviction. "For a man like Lee Church."

"I know you would."

Angie looked at his face and felt instant remorse for having just embarrassed him. This man wasn't a brute at all. He had only gotten swept up into a wayward set of bad circumstances. There wasn't a trace of meanness in him. She could see that now.

On impulse, Angie grabbed Ray's wrist and rose up on her tiptoes. She kissed his warm cheek.

"It's alright, Ray. Your Grampa explained everything."

Angie finally got into her car and carefully backed around the Bronco. She couldn't help but giggle at Ray, who was standing stock still, plastic bags hanging from both hands.

"Did your grandfather really hit that guy with his walking stick?"

"I'm afraid so."

"You and your grandfather need to settle down."

"It's way too late for Grampa."

"What about you? Maybe you should consider it."

"Settling down? That's what Kyla always tells me."

Ray watched Angie's tail lights disappear. In time, he heard muffled laughter coming from the sunporch. He turned to see Skinny and Paavo crowded together at a window, watching him. After being seen, they too disappeared from view.

"What were you old farts hee-hawing about?" Ray asked when he got inside.

"Your grandfather suggested we may need to go outside and pour water into your open mouth. He had concerns about your tongue drying up."

"Did you really say that, Grampa?"

"Oh, yeah. I say that."

"However, my main concern was for your clothing being soiled by roosting pigeons."

Paavo and Skinny laughed at one another's good humor. Both geezers were having a great time. Skinny kept up the razzing.

"The only token of affection I received was a little pat on the hand."

"I get a nice hug last night, but no kiss on the cheek."

Ray looked from one smug man to the other. He dumped the grocery bags on the dining room table.

"Apparently, you two don't have enough work to do. Why don't you put these away?"

Paavo hummed cheerfully as he sorted through the items on the table.

"What are you so happy about, Grampa?"

"We got everything going our way, Raymi."


Angie had a burst of inspiration and made one stop before going on to her parent's home. Jim and Lois were playing cribbage at the small table in the living room and they watched out the window as she pulled up in her car. Lois got up to retrieve Angie's lunch from the fridge so it could be re-heated in the microwave. Jim's curiosity peaked when he saw Angie rummaging around inside the trunk of her car. Whatever she took out, she kept it well-hidden, all the way into the house. She marched straight over to Jim and set the surprise on his lap. Lois came in from the kitchen.

"What in the world is this?"

"Looks like an artificial leg, Jim."

"I can certainly see that, Lois." Jim put on his reading glasses for a better look. "What's this about, Angie?"

"The knee joint came apart. I was hoping that it could be your next project…Geppetto." Angie and Lois grinned at Jim's newest name. "Do you think you can have it done by tomorrow morning?"

"How in the world would I know? I've never worked on anything like this."

"Well, Jim, then you'd better shake a leg."

"Yeah, Dad. I need you to put your best foot forward on this job."

Jim's eyes zipped back and forth between the two women.

"You two are simply hilarious."

Jim and Lois listened closely as Angie recited a lively account of her remarkable morning while slowly pecking away at her lasagna. Angie had to stop her meal several times as she and her mother giggled their way through the outrageous thermometer gag. They also got a good laugh out of Ray's bumpy, miserable ride back to the lodge.

Oh, and by the way, Roger would be just fine she told them. A scratched cornea was the main concern and the eye had been easily treated at the local clinic. She would only need to perform a quick follow-up exam tomorrow morning, and change the dressing on his injured arm.

Angie's excitement with the story waned noticeably when she told them about the clash in front of the lodge.

"Wow. A real fistfight?" Jim asked. "I didn't realize Ray had a temper."

"Everybody has a button they don't want pushed, Dad."

A tiny blip appeared on Lois' maternal radar screen. Her daughter had always expressed strong disapproval for any kind of over-aggression, no matter who was at fault. But this time she appeared to be defending it. Lois studied Angie with an appraising eye as she cleared the dishes from the table. Out in the kitchen, she thoughtfully poured herself a cup of coffee, wondering about Angie's sudden change of heart. She decided more information was needed. When Lois sat down at the table, Angie misjudged her mother's steady look for one of disapproval.

"Believe me, Mom. I was highly upset at first. It was awful. But then Grampa Maki explained why Ray got so upset. That's where the leg comes in."

Angie told them everything Paavo had said about the two instigators and of how an old family friend had paid the price for their shameful stupidity. Angie also repeated what Ray had said of Mr. Church and his war wounds. She skipped over the part about the kissing of Ray's cheek and finished up the long story with her car parked in the Church's driveway.

"Those poor people, they must have thought I was a little nutty when I asked for the leg." Angie laughed, "It took some convincing."

Lois intentionally rewound the story. She was probing.

"I'm a little shocked because Ray has always impressed me as a very laid-back person."

"Me, too." Jim agreed. "This whole fight thing is hard to imagine."

"Roger and Grampa Maki said more or less the same thing. And Ray told me that his brother-in-law tried to take the blame for all the trouble."

"So you've talked with Ray," Lois pointed out. "If I had to make a guess, I'd say he feels pretty bad about all this."

"He really did, Mom. You could see it on his face."

"What else did he say?"

"After all that craziness, the first thing he did was thank me for helping Roger. Then he apologized for taking up my whole morning."

"He said nothing about the fight?"

"Well, he did say he'd do it again." Angie quickly added, "But only if he was forced into it, I'm sure."

Lois made no further comment. Jim was already distracted by the leg next to him. He lifted it onto his lap.

"I know exactly what you're thinking, Mom. Ray should've turned the other cheek and walked away. But I won't blame him for what he did. Not under those circumstances."

"I don't blame him," Lois said in a neutral voice. "Not in the least."

Still, Angie felt the need to pile on more in her defense of Ray.

"You should have been there, Mom. After all that fuss, Ray even thought to bring ice cream for Roger." Angie leaned toward her mother and whispered, "I kissed him on the cheek for being so sweet. He blushed like a school kid."

Lois grinned at Angie's happy eyes. Her good mood disintegrated when she saw that Jim was totally engrossed with the leg on his lap.

"Did you hear any of that, Jim?"

"Yes." He didn't even bother to look up. "This thing is really old, but I think I can still make it work. Do you see here? The pivot pin was nearly worn through, that's why it broke."

Lois gave up and shrugged at Angie.

"If he wasn't so handy, I'd trade him in for a newer model."

Jim perked up, pulling partway out of his trance.

"You're absolutely right, Lois. The man deserves a newer model. He's a veteran, after all."

Lois and Angie each smothered a laugh as they looked at each other. Lois added in her well-practiced eye roll.

"It's like living with the Absent-Minded Professor…Oh, wait! That reminds me. The girls called."

"The girls! I've been so busy blabbing about Ray and everything, I almost forgot about them. I better call right away."

Lois watched Angie hurry to the phone. She took a sip of coffee and smiled. Her radar had been working perfectly.

# 10

Ray went to Disappointment Mountain. At least, that's the name he'd given it, after the death of his father. It wasn't a mountain at all, merely a pink granite bluff that guarded the entrance into the long and slender North Arm of Lost Woman Lake. The bare bedrock rose a scant eighteen feet above the water's surface, but at the time of the christening twenty years ago, the over-blown name seemed to fit.

Ray had found a way up the wall by pure accident and blind luck. Early one morning, less than a week after the funeral, he had stolen away with one of the resort's canoes, fully intending to disappear into the wild forever. He was nearly across the open water, heading for the northern arm and freedom from the hurt, when the warm September breeze was suddenly replaced by a cold, unrelenting wind. 'Canadian Clippers' his grandfather had called them. They were dangerous storms Ray knew, and he had fought the small gale for all he was worth; angling as best he could over the white-capped waves, straining toward the protection of the narrows until his teenage-arms ached so badly that the panicky effort brought tears to his eyes.

Ray never made it to the opening. He did, however, manage to point the canoe through the dense brush that grew along the base of the rock wall. It was there he pushed through and clutched onto the water-borne shrubs until the mostly-dry storm passed over some twenty minutes later. The fast-moving cold front had almost accomplished what Ray never really meant to have happen; wipe him off the face of the earth, never to be seen again.

The sharp, grit-filled wind died as quickly as it had appeared and when Ray could finally open his eyes completely he noticed a thin-lipped, irregular stairway up the fractured bedrock. His courage and strength back, the challenge of such a climb was irresistible. Once at the top of the short summit, Ray sat on his newfound perch for a long time, legs dangling over the edge as he ate breakfast from his backpack, enjoying his own private view of the lake. He was having an unexpectedly good time until he saw his grandfather paddling toward him in a worn-out, wooden canoe. Ray tried to hide himself behind a small pine tree at the back of the ledge but it was too late, he'd been spotted.

He had anticipated the worst sort of punishment from Paavo, especially after ignoring his grandfather's calls and forcing the old man to scale the tricky wall. But Ray was mistaken. No punishment was handed out and he ended up being pleasantly surprised by Grampa's quiet understanding - not to mention his climbing skills. They had talked long into the morning and, although Ray didn't realize it at the time, their get-together on the bluff was an important turning point in his young life. From that morning on, Ray honestly felt in his heart that he wasn't all alone in the world, and that Grampa was a special man. A man you could always count on. Just like Dad. After that day, each solitary visit he had made to this spot held some unique meaning for him, and him alone. This hard granite retreat had been his soft place of refuge during the uncertainty of his teenage years.

For now, Ray rested his back against the familiar trunk of the lonely-looking Jack Pine. He remembered back to the last time he had stopped here at this open hideaway, more than fifteen years ago; the morning of the day he'd left home for boot camp. At eighteen years of age, Ray had been both nervous and excited about leaving, very much wanting to prove himself to a larger slice of the world, yet already feeling homesick. Serving in the army had been a good experience for Ray and during his three-year hitch he had grown into a full-fledged man. After returning home, he had never felt the need or the inclination to come back to Disappointment Mountain. Until now. Something in his life had changed. Somehow, and he wasn't sure why, he'd been drawn here again.

On today's visit, Ray's old mountain sensed no disappointment coming from him. In point of fact, Ray was doing pretty well considering all the morning upheaval. Earlier, while paddling over here, before even putting a foot on the first narrow step of the cliff face, Ray had decided to waste no more time thinking about the fight. It was over and done, move on.

Ordinarily, Ray would have carried a gut-load of shame in the aftermath of such a public display. In truth, though, Ray was damn proud of himself. He knew there wasn't a better reason or a better man to fight for than Mr. Church - well, other than Grampa. And while he'd gotten no pleasure from dishing out the punishment, Ray did feel those two puddin' heads had gotten everything they deserved. Mr. Church was absolutely right; those men had come knocking at his old door, not the other way around. So it was easy for Ray to put that troubled part of the morning behind him. The only misgivings he had were how much he had upset his family. He hoped they would think no less of him.

Ray reached out, gathered up a handful of withered pine cones, and one by one, tossed them over the cliff edge. He paid little attention to the beautiful view or to the sporadic line of vacationers who funneled their laden canoes past him and into the narrows below. From there, these hearty sightseers would cross the full length of the mile-long arm of Lost

Woman, to Chippewa Portage, one of the main points that would gain them further entry into the BWCA. After toting their gear and canoes over the sixteen-rod span of the old trail, users of the park could camp, fish, and portage all the way into Canada, given the right amount of ambition and proper paperwork. Ray had done it countless times.

A female loon nudged her way into Ray's quiet session when she swam into the periphery of his view. He watched from his overhead perch as she tended closely to a fluffy pair of babies. The little ones were having great fun swimming small, daring circles around their nervous mother. Before very long an unseen threat caught the attention of the overly-cautious mom and Ray smiled when the infant puffballs clambered onto her safe back after heeding her invisible warning. Ray searched the lake for signs of the male bird but father loon was nowhere around. He hoped nothing bad had happened because that would make things tougher on the female. Ray looked back to the loon family and saw one of the chicks had gotten back into the water. Whatever had been wrong, the danger had apparently passed. The second chick continued freeloading a ride on mom's back, and soon, they were gone from his sight.

Probably just trying to get warm, Ray thought. Or maybe that chick was the weaker of the two and needed some extra help. That happened sometimes; a runt or a straggler in the brood would require more attention than what was normal. Ray hoped that wasn't the case because Mother Nature had a way of weeding out those who didn't measure up to her standards.

Ray tensed, and he sat up straighter. A straggler...who needed extra attention...like him. The eerie similarity was hard to ignore - a missing father, a nervous mother burdened with a dawdler. Ray tried steering his thoughts in another direction but the comparison began to fit him like a glove - an immature freeloader, who relied too much on the family's good will. Ray's self-perceptions spiraled downward, into a harsh, overly-critical assessment of himself.

He really was a freeloader; the only one in his family who hadn't taken on a fair share of responsibility. He'd left Ma and Kyla to take up the slack. He was the friendly bystander of the family who acted more like the hired help. Oh, he was likeable enough, but not someone to be taken seriously.

And he didn't measure up, either. Not like the men he had known, like Dad and Mr. Church. And Grampa. They were strong men, always able to face-up to tough times. Skinny had confirmed that time and again during their talks. The old hermit had said men like John Maki and Lee Church were unequaled in character, as were so many of the men of that era. That those men, having outlasted a Great Depression, had also been called upon to fight in a war that saved an entire world from tyranny. Skinny had said that no generation since, has ever measured up to those standards.

Ray felt the delayed sting of the old hermit's words and took them to heart. Ray Maki wasn't the kind of man you could count on. He'd already proven that because every single time in his past, when his own character had been tested, he had turned the other way. And here he was again, thirty-three years old and back at his hiding spot, still running away like an immature kid. The only thing missing was his Grampa coming to save him.

Then all at once, Ray saw the frightened boy who had fled to this place twenty years ago. In his mind, he pictured the young teenage kid who had bared his soul to his grandfather while pleading for God to send his father back home, alive and well. Ray could see that tearful boy clearly, holding on to an old man; clinging to the impossible hope of an unanswerable prayer.

How very sad.

Ray looked away from the blue water to the white knuckles of his clenched fists, surprised to see they were tightened up in such a strong way. He was hanging on for dear life again, grasping on to God knows what this time.

And then the realization hit him. Ray suddenly knew what was clasped in his hands because he'd been holding on to it for twenty long years.

It was Dad. Ray had him in a long-distance death grip.

He opened his hands.

When he let go, Ray's severe self-judgments eventually disappeared, leaving his life in a truer light. He understood, rightly this time, that he had let a large part of his life get mired down by deliberately keeping a foot in the past, searching for the missing goodbye that had been denied him twenty years earlier. He had gotten stuck, rummaging around in times gone by, forever looking for the closure that was never there. He couldn't even bring himself to part with a beat-up Bronco. Talk about hanging on.

Worse than that, Ray reflected, he had been too unaware to even notice his half-hearted attempt at living his own life. He had only gone through the empty motions, pretending at life, but never really feeling the true rewards.

Everyone else in the family had gone forward; taking on responsibilities as they went ahead; expanding, along with their growing lives, and most importantly...accepting. Accepting the good, and the bad, of what life cast their way. Everyone had moved on. Everybody but him.

"What a bonehead."

Until this moment, Ray had never fully understood that the last twenty years had not belonged only to him. He had willingly shared those years with an old, heavy memory that had kept him anchored in the same unchanging spot, leaving him to run in place for nearly two decades.

Ray looked skyward and he pushed out a long sigh. Shaking his head from side to side, Ray told himself, to once and for all, let John Maki rest in peace.

He rose to his feet.

"Gotta go, Dad."

Finally, at long last, Ray's slow race to nowhere…ended.

Ray stared at the lonely pine that had touched his back and mirrored his life. A stunted tree, stubbornly hanging on to a solitary life atop a barren rock ledge. A simple-minded tree, totally surrounded by the fullness of life, blissfully unaware of its own isolation.

Disgusted with himself, Ray turned his back to the lonesome pine and walked to the cliff's edge, ready to leave. He stopped short.

Of all the extraordinary events that had happened on this singular day, Ray found it strange that Kyla's words now found their way into his head.

"You'll end up like Skinny," she had said, "just you and a stupid dog."

"Well, maybe me and the stupid dog part," Ray said out loud.

It was a glib answer to a careless statement made by a caring sister. But unlike all the other times Kyla had poked into his personal business, this time Ray really did understand her sisterly concern for him. She'd only wanted more for her brother. She wanted him to lead a richer, fuller life by allowing himself to love, and be loved. Kyla was dead-on with her dismal forecast for his future. And Ray now knew it.

Angie was also right. As she had said in her snap evaluation of Skinny, Ray realized that, he too, had been holding most people at arm's length, trying very hard to spare himself the trouble of any further heartbreaking disappointments. He, like Skinny Severson, kept a small, safe cluster of people around him, allowing no one else to enter his constricted life. Though not entirely so, he was a lot like Skinny. More than he had ever imagined.

With that not-so-gentle push from Kyla, coupled with Angie's sharp analysis of an old hermit, Ray found his way to the heart of why he had been drawn here and what had changed in his life. After an entire afternoon's worth of circling the issue, Ray finally admitted to what had happened to him the first time he stared into the prettiest set of green eyes he'd ever seen.

He had fallen in love…first look.

"Funny deal."

Well to the south, Ray caught sight of the towering pines belonging to Pike Point. He immediately thought of his grandfather.

Maybe the old man was right. Maybe some things that happened in life weren't just the results of dumb luck. Like Ma and Mr. Church coming here, so many years ago. Grampa had always believed that all of them ending up together was supposed to happen. As if their arrival was preordained, or something. But how could Grampa know that for sure? How could anybody? All that kind of talk was probably just his old-time way of thinking - a peculiar leftover, from the Old Country.

But still, when you thought about more, it was hard to overlook everything that had happened in the last two days, because so much of it seemed aimed directly at him. And if you viewed things Grampa's way, his old logic made some sense. At least, more than it ever had before.

If any of that superstitious stuff was true, then maybe Angie was here for more than a simple visit, or than to merely patch up a touchy hermit.

"Enkeli," Ray whispered. "I guess we'll find out, Grampa."

Paavo and Skinny were seated together on the double swing when Ray paddled up alongside his dock. He carried the canoe well up on shore and carefully rolled it over, belly up. After leaning both paddles against its bottom, Ray walked over and sat on the opposite bench, across from the two men.

"You go to your mountain?" Paavo asked right away.

"You never miss a trick, do you?"

"I pay attention, that's all."

Out of the clear blue, Ray asked, "How come you never got married again, Grampa?"

Skinny started to get up. Paavo touched his arm and stopped him from leaving. He answered Ray's question without embarrassment; one of life's modest rewards for having reached old age.

"My Augusta be the kind of woman who gives everything to me. So I do the same for her. After she die, there be nothing left for anyone else." Paavo added, "Ellie be that way, too."

The old man had jumped ahead of Ray, already answering the next question.

"Why do you ask that, Raymi?"

"I don't know, Grampa. Just wondering."

Skinny quietly joined in.

"Perhaps the unusual events prompted some timely soul-searching."

"You don't miss much either."

"I must confess. You have been the subject of our discussion for the better part of the afternoon."

"And?"

"Your grandfather and I have taken separate paths to arrive at the same conclusion. And that is, you are a genuinely decent, well-intentioned man, who at certain times seems to lack the little sense that God gave the average goose."

"Thanks a lot, Skinny," Ray chuckled, taking no offense.

"Think nothing of it…Now make of it what you will."

Ray looked from one man to the other.

"I take it you guys are referring to Angie…Right?"

"A tad slow on the uptake, but well done, Mr. Maki."

Paavo grabbed onto Skinny's wrist.

"I always like the way you speak. Like a professional man."

"Many thanks, my old friend." Skinny's eye-patch wrinkled up as he smiled. "And you, Paavo Maki, are the salt of the earth."

# 11

ANGIE FELT DISAPPOINTED. SHE HAD hoped to speak with Ray during the morning house call but he was nowhere to be found. Her extra fussing about hair, make-up, and clothing had been for naught, other than seeming to amuse her mother. But Skinny was on the mend and that fact tempered away any letdown from not finding Ray at home.

Her morning had started out well. She had stopped at the Church household and presented the repaired leg to a gracious Janine. Angie had also given her the name and telephone number of an orthopedic specialist who made bi-weekly visits to the Veteran's Clinic in Duluth. Carefully, and delicately, Angie had urged the quiet woman to make an appointment, telling her the prosthesis was out-dated and her husband would be amazed by the great strides that field of medicine had taken in recent years. Janine Church had smiled shyly at the accidental gaff and assured a mildly embarrassed Angie she would do her best to point out that fact to her husband.

"I've mentioned the subject before," she had said. "I'll certainly try again, although, my husband tends to have a mind of his own."

Angie had sensed during their brief meeting, that one way or another, the velvet-voiced woman could get her husband to do whatever was best for him. She had driven away feeling very good.

On the sofa in Ray's sunporch Angie sat near Skinny, both of them relaxing in the pent-up warmth of the early morning. The old hermit had showered and shaved, in spite of the eye patch, and his color had returned. His stark-white, walrus moustache stood out sharply against his light brown skin. He wore a bright-red, Lost Woman sweatshirt and a spanking new pair of dungarees. Cleaned up the way he was, the old curmudgeon bordered on handsome.

And Roger had surprised her by being so chatty. She had expected something totally different. Evidently she'd passed muster, and had been accepted into his tight world. Ray was absolutely right; this was a highly-intelligent, remarkably articulate man. Skinny's many questions pertaining to her particular branch of medical profession were pointed, incisive, and well thought out, as though he were measuring the depth of her knowledge. Angie found herself responding carefully, monitoring her answers, feeling a bit like she was being given an oral exam. Conversation with this man was no lighthearted affair. Angie needed to stay on her toes and pay close attention, if she wanted to keep up her end of the bargain. Angie believed herself to be in the company of an extraordinarily bright man. She was enjoying the experience thoroughly.

After completing a wordy examination and a dressing change on her well-spoken patient, Angie found herself wanting to stay in the sunporch. She felt no need to rush off.

Bridget and Maggie head-butted their noisy way through a doggie door and Skinny ordered them to hush up. Like scolded children, they solemnly followed his orders, and his pointing finger, into the next room. They lay down together on Maggie's oversized bed.

"When do you expect Ray?"

Skinny paused, frowning at her, seeming to glean hidden meaning from the inquiry. Angie regretted having asked the question.

"Our good friend will be returning near the lunch hour. He informed me that a warm meal was to be expected upon his arrival. A tasty meal I am sure, prepared by his mother. Afterward, Bridget and I will be on our way...with your permission of course."

"Permission granted."

Angie smiled at the formality. She suspected Skinny would do whatever he damn well pleased. He was only being polite for her benefit.

"A warm meal, that's nice of Ellie."

"Ellen possesses an exceptional kindness. I expected no less from a woman such as her." Skinny added, "That quality runs throughout the entire Maki family, despite the aberration you and I witnessed yesterday.

"Still feeling the need to defend Ray?" Angie teased. "If you are, you may have to get in line."

"Ray hardly needs my assistance. Nevertheless, if what you have said about getting in line is true, you have also reinforced my so-called defense of him."

"I guess I did."

Skinny faced directly toward Angie.

"Allow me one question, in order that I may make a point."

"Go on."

"How, may I ask, were you able to drum up enough courage to venture out into the wilderness and come to the aid of a person whom you knew not at all?

"Actually, I said no when Ray first called. I was uncomfortable with the idea...to say the least."

"Yet you came, even though you were accompanied by someone with whom you've had little or no previous contact."

"My parents have known Ray for a while."

"So, some *one*, or some *thing*, obviously changed your mind."

Skinny waited patiently for a response. Unlike yesterday, while at his house, today the uneasy shoe was on her foot. Feeling the pressure, Angie confessed like a guilty witness on the stand.

"It was my Dad. He said Ray was good people."

"Ahh, to my point." Skinny buttoned up his remarks using a clever tactic. "I have never met your father, although it appears he has excellent judgment."

"He does."

Skinny had presented his case like a lawyer furthering an argument. Angie shifted in place and brushed away some unseen lint from her neatly-pressed slacks.

Skinny thought he spotted another opportunity.

"You are very well dressed for a casual house call."

Angie was immediately relieved. Skinny had gone a bridge too far.

"I'm going to late-morning Mass with my parents," she answered with a good-natured grin. "As soon as you're finished with the interrogation."

"My apologies, Angelica, if I have crossed a line that *you* don't want crossed. I can be overly abrasive at times."

"No offense taken, Roger." She added, "Though you did have me wondering where you earned your law degree."

"History is my major." He leaned closer. "You and I share the same alma mater."

Skinny stopped short and pulled back.

"Enough of me." He quickly switched back to Angie. "I would expect you and your parents have big plans for the remainder of your holiday."

"Not really. Tomorrow, Dad wants to go on a tour of an old underground mine that's somewhere around here. He said it would be fun but Mom and I are not totally convinced. It sounded pretty scary to us."

"Your father is correct, again. The Soudan Underground is a fascinating tour. You will plunge more than two thousand feet down into the bowels of the earth where hardy men were in search of hematite, the richest iron ore ever found in this part of the world; ore that helped feed an industrial revolution, and two world wars."

"Well, no need to go now, I feel like I've already taken the tour."

Angie had tried teasing him a second time. The effort fell flat. She made a mental note not to do it anymore. Some people were just that way; they didn't see the humor in it. Roger, she was happy to see, overlooked the offense.

"Paavo was once employed at that particular mine, some seventy-odd years ago."

"I'll make sure to tell Dad before we go on the tour. He really enjoyed meeting Grampa Maki."

"Indeed, Paavo is an exceptional man."

Angie glanced at her watch and then picked up one of the two bags next to her on the sofa.

"A couple things, Roger, then I've got to run. The clinic was nice enough to supply you with extra gauze and bandages. Please use them until your arm is sufficiently healed."

"Bandages supplied at your request, no doubt."

"Well, yes. But they're not a total freebie, you'll be charged a little something for them." Angie handed over the second bag. "And this is also for you. I guessed at the sizes."

Skinny looked inside the second bag. He pulled out a three-pack of sleeveless white tee-shirts and a new flannel shirt.

"Charity, Angelica? There is no need." Skinny seemed genuinely upset. "I do well enough. Thank you for the gesture."

He carefully put the shirts back into the bag. Angie refused to take it back.

"Please don't think of this as charity, Roger. Accept them in the spirit in which they are given. As a gift, to a newfound friend."

Skinny set the package on his lap.

"Well said." With an appreciative smile, he added, "Apparently, the Maki clan does not have a corner on the kindness market."

Bridget was extremely happy to be home. As soon as Skinny opened the door of the Bronco she was off his lap and broadcasting her arrival. The scrappy little bulldog made up for lost time, darting here and sniffing there, as she went about the crucial assignment of scurrying away any uninvited pests from her clearly defined territory. Aware that all eyes were trained on her, she paced back and forth near the house. Then, with a menacing growl, and a quick look to her small audience, Bridget disappeared into the crawl space under the house. Maggie whined jealously from the truck box.

"Stay," Ray commanded firmly. "Better mind your own business."

"A valuable lesson most everyone ought to learn."

"Including me?"

"Misguided as your actions were, they were intended for my good," Skinny said seriously. "My behavior was also in question. Let us leave the entire episode where it belongs, in the past."

"Fair enough," Ray said.

Both men were satisfied. No exchanging of apologies was necessary.

Once they entered the house, Ray helped stow away the supplies which still sat in boxes near the washstand. When they finished, Skinny scribbled at the bottom of a pre-made supply order. Ray thought it best to say nothing when he noticed Skinny had added peanut butter to the list.

"Is that everything?" Ray asked, slipping the paper into a shirt pocket.

"No, not quite." Skinny pointed to the high-backed chair. "Have a seat, Ray."

"Sure."

Skinny went to the corner bunk, dropped to his knees and slid out a leather-bound trunk that was stashed beneath. While the old hermit busied himself by carefully pulling small items from the chest, Ray sat down and studied the carving that was clamped to the table in front of him. The close up view revealed even finer details of the Skinny's skills. It truly was a work of sculptured art.

But something about the wood figure seemed different today. Somehow, when viewed from this angle, Skinny's angle, the loon appeared to strike a totally different pose. Gone from the bird was the raised-up defiance and fighting spirit he had first envisioned two days ago. Today, from his new perspective, Ray thought the loon to be panicked, and terribly desperate, locked in a hopeless struggle, and straining with all of its strength to break free from the uncarved block of wood that held both feet prisoner.

"Weird," Ray thought.

He shifted uncomfortably in the chair.

"Ahh, here we are." Both men got to their feet. "I have a special request, Ray."

From a homemade felt sleeve, Skinny pulled out a beautifully carved Diamond Willow cane. He regarded his work with a trained eye and then handed it to Ray. The multiple, dark brown diamonds had been hollowed out and sanded smooth. Rounded-off ridges surrounded each elongated diamond, making them stand out sharply from the pale yellow of the stick. At the top, a knotted deformity in the wood made for an off-set sphere that fit perfectly into the palm of Ray's hand. The tapered bottom had been tipped with a polished brass fitting. In military script, the old man had burnt - AA 82$^{nd}$ Airborne - into the lighter colored wood. The deep finish glowed in Ray's hand.

"The connected double-A signifies 'All American'," Skinny said.

"I remember what you told me. All fifty states." Ray asked, "For Mr. Church, right?"

"Yes, by way of your father." Skinny explained, "Shortly before he passed, John found this particular piece of willow in a nearby swamp. He asked if I would then carve it into a cane for Lee Church. Afterward, when the cane was completed, I could not bring myself to present it to Lee. I…ahh, I have always had a certain lack of expression when it comes to some types of strong emotions."

"So you want me to give this to him?"

"Along with my heartfelt respect for his brave service and great sacrifice."

"Mr. Church will love it, Skinny. Dad would've, too. Thank you."

Skinny turned away quickly. He went to his knees again and started putting away the items he had placed on the floor. He stopped in mid-packing when he lifted up an ornately-framed photograph. Skinny permitted himself a few private seconds to stare at the young woman in the photo, before speaking to Ray.

"As you know too well, Mr. Maki, fate can be a fickle mistress. On this occasion, however, her timing appears flawless."

Ray couldn't have agreed more. He slipped the cane back into the sleeve and walked quietly out the door.

# 12

THIS TIME A PHONE CALL would not be good enough. Ray needed to see her face, to see her reaction, first hand. Then he would know. He had purposely kept away for three days, unsure but hoping he was doing the right thing. In a couple minutes he would find out.

Ray had thrown himself into his work during that time, arriving early, staying late, keeping as busy as he could, which really wasn't a hard thing to do. All of the extra effort had helped distract him from thinking of Angie too much. There was also the added bonus of seeing Kyla's surprised face the three mornings he had shown up for work, on time and clean-shaven. If Kyla wondered what was going on, she never said a word. But Ray could see that his sister was dying to know the reason for his change of habits. She was just too stubborn to ask. He was enjoying her little dilemma.

All three of the Holters turned his way at the sound of the Bronco's clunky approach. When they all recognized who was coming, he saw Jim bend down to put a hand on the top rung of the scaffolding, springing himself to the ground like a man half his age. Lois balanced a long length of cedar siding on a saw table, a dusty pair of goggles perched on top of her head. But it was Angie's reaction that caused him to smile.

As nonchalantly as she could, Ray watched her climb down off the platform, take off a weighty nail apron and then enter the house. He was fairly sure she'd gone inside to straighten up her appearance. And if that was true, he was off to a good start. If she didn't care what he thought, she wouldn't have bothered.

"Come for the canoe?" Jim asked after Ray got out of his truck.

"Not today. Afternoon, Lois."

"Hi, Ray. What's up?"

"I came to thank Jim and Angie for all they did for Mr. Church. He's back walking again."

"That's good to hear," Lois said, slipping off the goggles.

"It was an easy fix, but temporary." Jim said. "The pivot pin needed replacing. Took only five minutes at the hardware store to find something that would work."

"Mrs. Church called three days ago," Angie said from the porch steps.

As she made her way over toward them, Ray saw that he had guessed right. She had run a brush through her hair and put on a touch of fresh lipstick. And more than likely, Ray presumed, she also had to dab away some perspiration from her face. It was a hot afternoon. Ray thought she looked just right in her dark-blue tee-shirt and worn out jeans he had first seen her wearing when he drove up. Evidently, she wasn't willing to go through a change of clothes for him. But then, that would have been too obvious - to everyone.

"If your Dad can spare you for a couple minutes, I'd like to talk to you."

"How about it, boss? Do I have time for a break?"

"Yeah, let's all go down to the boathouse."

"Come in the cabin, Jim," Lois said. "I'll get you a lemonade."

"I just had one."

"Come inside and have another."

"I wanted to show Ray the canoe. It's all done."

"Angie can show him."

"But..."

"Inside, Einstein." Lois rolled her eyes at Angie.

After Lois ushered Jim into the house, Angie took the lead to the boathouse. She stopped at the door.

"You promised not to pester me anymore."

"I lied. I do it all the time. Can't seem to help myself."

"I'll have to remember that."

Angie flipped the light switch and the old canoe gleamed into Ray's view. He went to it immediately, putting his hands on the upper edging. It looked better than he had ever imagined.

"Oh, man, this is unbelievable. I never expected anything this good. I can hardly wait for Grampa to see it."

And Angie could hardly wait to tell her Dad. She knew Jim had spent the better part of last winter reworking the old craft. She was pleased to see Ray admire the workmanship of her father.

Ray ran his hands all along the canoe. Angie watched his boyish reaction and couldn't help but agree with her father. Ray was good people. He was an open, straightforward guy who showed not a trace of phony pretense. What you saw is what you got. His soft-spoken reserve was genuine, and very appealing. It added to his good looks.

Angie found herself smiling along with Ray when he squatted down and lightly touched his fingers on the white lettering: P. Maki Guiding.

"What are you going to do with it?" she asked.

"I'm going to hang it from the rafters of the lodge. You know, tipped open at an angle. I'll put it right above the fireplace."

Angie visualized the canoe high in the corner, suspended from the vaulted ceiling of the dining area, and canted a little, so you could see the inside wood. She approved of the placement, and the intended tribute to Grampa Maki.

"I told my Dad it should be on display somewhere. He'll like your idea a lot."

Ray stood up, leaving little distance between them.

"Actually, there's one more reason why I came over here."

Angie said nothing. She liked him being so close.

"Wednesday's are always the slowest day at the resort so I usually take that morning off. I'd like to take you on a tour of the lake, and maybe we could catch a couple fish for a shore lunch, if you want."

"I would love to go but I can't," Angie said sadly. "I'm leaving early tomorrow morning."

"Then maybe the next time you're here."

If Ray was disappointed, he didn't show it. He seemed unfazed by the turndown, accepting her at her word. Angie felt obligated to explain.

"I have two nursing students who rent rooms from me. I promised them I would be home by tomorrow afternoon. They have finals on Friday and wanted me to help with their studying…I'm sorry, Ray. I would have loved to go."

"Like I said, catch you next time."

"The Fourth," Angie said quickly. "I was thinking about coming back on the Fourth of July weekend."

"Well, I don't think that's going to work out. Kyla said the Fourth is on a Saturday this year, so the resort will be pretty busy that weekend."

Angie was genuinely dismayed. Until she saw his grin. He was teasing her. She liked that.

"We always add extra help for holiday weekends. As far as I'm concerned, we have a date."

"We'll see," she teased back. "The Fourth is a long way off, maybe I'll forget."

"I sure won't."

The sincerity in his voice brought an instant halt to their lighthearted exchange, leaving them all alone in the quiet heat of the small building. For a moment, with their eyes linked together, something in Ray's expression seemed to pull her forward. She averted her eyes, but quickly looked at him again. She liked the serious look she saw on his face. She also liked the feeling of being in his presence.

And then Angie did something she had never done. She kissed first. She was immediately happy she had because Ray responded just right; not too hard, or too pushy, or trying to take control of their embrace. He was gauging his kiss to hers. She liked that very much. She also liked the way he kept looking at her when the kiss was over. It left her with tingling goose bumps.

"The Fourth," she said. "For sure."

# 13

Someone had once told Angie that the road leading into Hell was paved with good intentions. She was reminded of the saying when the tiny Cross of her necklace rose up with wind and tapped lightly against the bottom of her chin. Up until that point she had thought everything would be okay; that she would be able to work her way out of this tight spot. But after the necklace thing, she wasn't so sure anymore.

Angie slid forward on the seat and let her knees drop to the bottom edges of the canoe, automatically lowering her profile and allowing for better leverage. Dropping lower down was a natural reaction to the rolling unsteadiness, and it helped. She was able to stabilizer herself and dig deeper into the water with her paddle. The old craft responded to her newfound power. For a while, Angie was making decent headway, and Pike Point soon seemed within reach.

"I can make it," she thought.

The honest truth was, her chances were not very good.

Angie's morning, like all her mornings, had been filled with normal, everyday decisions, nothing too important or earth shattering. Unfortunately, most of those decisions had been the wrong ones. At the time, though, Angie had no way of knowing those trivial choices would stack up against her. Not until it was too late.

If she had only listened to the little voice in her head that had warned her to keep hugging the shoreline. Then she would be safe now. But the lure of getting a close-up photo of a mother loon carrying her downy babies on her back had been too enticing to pass up. The innate charm of the feathery trio had drawn her into open water, aided by the benign breeze at her back. Angie would have stopped altogether had she known she was chasing the little family away from the leeward side of the Point. She had gotten distracted, unaware of how far she had drifted out into the big lake.

At the beginning of the innocent pursuit, the westerly breeze had been merely a nuisance, barely ruffling Angie's hair. What's more, she hadn't even gotten the photo she'd wanted. The birds were too wary and speedy to allow for the opportunity of a decent snapshot. After grudgingly giving up on the idea, Angie had turned the canoe around only to witness the warm breeze give way to a stiff wind. When she saw the near-black clouds push past the treetops ahead of her, the small lump of anxiety in her throat had yielded to an overall dread.

Had Angie been a little more experienced in outdoor matters she would have understood the scope and scale of the oncoming threat. Then she would have chosen differently. She would have headed in the opposite direction, for the protection of a distant island where she could wait out the storm, like the mother loon now had in mind. Somehow, unlike Angie, the adult bird had known what was coming.

In what seemed like a matter of seconds, the leading edge of the cold front had plowed away every hint of the warm morning, rapidly changing the lake into a roiling mass of dark-gray water. The blue sky had disappeared completely, into a scary, whistling gloom. Once sensing the power of what she was up against, Angie had to will away the fear that threatened to overwhelm her. Giving in to panic would do no good. That basic lesson had been drummed into her at the start of nursing school.

As conditions steadily worsened, Angie wished she had just gotten into her car and left for St. Paul, like she had planned all along. Her last minute idea of having Ray and her father pose in the restored canoe seemed silly and ridiculous now. All of this was a bad mistake and none of it should be happening. She should have just gone home.

But wishing away the uproar in front of her was useless thinking. Her situation was desperately real and no amount of regret would change things. To her credit, Angie let go of the worthless thoughts and concentrated on her paddling. She did her best to ignore the cold sprays of lake water that soaked her clothes and skin every time the heavy wood canoe slapped against the rising waves. Angie alternated her paddling from side to side and tried her best to keep the canoe faced directly into the wind. Common sense dictated she could not get thrown sideways. Then the waves would wash over the low-slung sides, and sink her. And there was no way she'd be able to swim to shore, not in this freezing, mixed-up mess of a lake.

After five minutes of fighting the wind and the waves, Angie's arms and shoulders burned from the effort. She ignored that, too. She leaned forward to relieve the pain in her lower back and then narrowed her eyes to the grit carried on the wind. Right now, Angie did not dare think of how bad she was hurting, or how grim the situation looked. She just pulled hard, time after time, determined not to go down without a damn good fight.

Ray had slept in late. At seven o'clock, Maggie could stand it no longer so she nudged at his hand, wondering with her sad-looking eyes why breakfast had not been served. The wet-nose prodding had awakened

Ray from a peaceful sleep and after some good-natured grumbling, he shuffled to the kitchen and fed her the usual half-can of Friskies dog chow. Ray went outside to the sunporch steps and waited for her to finish eating. Within seconds, Maggie popped out of her doggie door and nosed at his hand for the after-meal treat he held in his palm.

"Sit."

Maggie heeded his order and vibrated in place.

"You or Jag, I don't know who eats faster."

He threw Maggie's dessert toward the lake and the dog went after the fake bone as though she hadn't eaten in weeks. She flopped down and chomped at the treat where it landed, and none too quietly. She returned shortly and sat obediently at Ray's side, in hopes her good manners would result in more goodies.

"Jag eats a little slower than you, but he makes more noise."

Ray laughed at his own humor. He'd have to remember to use the gag on his brother-in-law. Kyla and the boys would like it, too.

It was an unusually warm morning so Ray walked to the end of his dock clad only in gray sweatpants and white socks. Maggie double-checked the area where she had devoured her treat, sniffing the ground thoroughly, in case she'd missed a crunchy crumb.

No such luck.

To the north, halfway between his dock and the end of the Point, Ray spotted the same mother loon he had seen during his Saturday visit to the bluff. She and her two chicks were milling about, with no perceived purpose, and not straying very far from shore. Ray watched them for a while and puzzled over their aimless wanderings. He concluded that she must be teaching them some type of necessary lesson, but what it was, he did not know. Maggie couldn't figure it out, either.

Ray checked the lake for any sign of the male bird but he was nowhere around. After failing to spot father loon, Ray cut short his lake-watching ritual and went inside the cabin to take a shower. He dressed in jeans and a tee, then shaved for a personal best, fifth morning in a row. He went back to the kitchen to prepare a bag lunch that he immediately stuffed into his backpack. It was a perfect morning to be out on the lake, even though he would be alone today.

"Nothing new there," he thought.

Ray no sooner plugged in the coffee maker when he heard the wind whistle through the screen of his back door. He opened it and looked out to the west sky. The coolness was unexpected.

"Crap," he said, deflated by the change in weather.

He decided to go on as planned. The fast-moving clouds looked as though they would blow over in a hurry.

Against Lois' wishes, Jim had gotten into the car and drove away, ignoring her request to allow Angie and Ray some time alone. He was simply too excited to wait. He had really liked Angie's idea of taking a photo with him and Ray sitting in the old canoe. Jim already had big plans to enlarge and then frame the photograph, once Angie got the film developed. He had even picked out an open spot on a wall in the living room - with Lois' approval, of course. The picture would be a nice thing to look at from time to time. A happy reminder of all his hard work and Angie's first visit to Lost Woman.

So, like an over-eager kid on Christmas morning, Jim grinned from ear to ear and rushed to his reward.

"Please, not like this."

If Angie was pleading to the wind, it mattered not because the small gale harbored no ill intentions toward her. On the other hand, it would also show her no mercy. The sudden storm rushing over her was merely a force of nature, blind and unfeeling to any one or any thing in its path. There was no wrath or fury involved in the storm's existence, even though it sometimes seemed that way. If harm or suffering was an end result of its passing, well, nothing personal.

After all, wind happened. Storms did, too. So Angie being caught out on the lake was simply unfortunate timing. She happened to be in the wrong place at the wrong time; a hapless casualty of rare circumstances.

Life was like that sometimes.

Angie knew all that because she had often seen the suffering caused from ill-timed events. Like the undeserved pain inflicted on the victims of a drunk driver. Or the tragic deaths of a young family trapped by a chance house fire. The intention to hurt, or to punish, was always absent. And no hard feelings were aimed at those unlucky targets of a sad fate. Angie was painfully aware that innocent people frequently died at the hands of random bad luck because she had often witnessed life's sorrowful endings.

Death was like that sometimes.

Still, Angie never thought anything like this would come smashing down onto her safe world. But then, who did?

Angie hoped against all odds that her expensive camera wasn't getting damaged but she didn't dare take her eyes away from the high-cresting waves to look down and check on its welfare. She could, however, feel the cold water flowing back and forth past her knees and ankles every time the canoe rose up to meet the sharp swells. She felt very bad because the camera was a high school graduation gift from her parents, and now it was probably ruined. Angie tried once again to clear away the useless thoughts. She needed to direct her efforts on the impossible task in front of her.

But she was nearing the limits of her endurance so her mind kept wandering. Like the relentless waves in front of her, the unwanted thoughts found a way to keep on coming.

Mom and Dad would be devastated. Angie said a quick prayer for them, so they would be able to move on, past her dying. She did not want them to mourn over her. She only wanted them to remember in their hearts that they had always done their best for her. And thanks to them she'd always been very happy. Angie would miss them dearly. They were good people.

In her mind's eye Angie saw their intolerably sad faces, weeping together for their cold and wet, lifeless daughter. It was a chilling image too depressing to even consider and when it stayed a millisecond too long, Angie drove the vision from her head.

"No!" she screamed. "Not like this!"

Angie set her jaw and decided she would not give up. She would keep on fighting, for no matter how long. Not for herself, for Mom and Dad.

The loud pounding on the sunporch door made Ray jump and Maggie bark. He left his coffee cup on the kitchen counter to see who was doing the banging. With the wind like it was, he hadn't heard anyone pull into the driveway. Neither had Maggie, she had been snoring too loud. Through the windows of the sunporch, Ray saw Jim Holter running back from the dock, to the cabin again. Even from a distance, Ray could see that his face looked drawn and tight. He looked scared, shaken to the core. Something had to be very wrong. Ray met him at the door as Jim pointed to the lake.

"Angie. She was bringing the canoe…"

Ray shoved past him and ran toward his dock. He instantly caught sight of Angie, about two hundred yards out and a little to the north, bobbing wildly with the heavy waves. Ray was thrilled to see she was still afloat. He had assumed she was already in the water. Considering the size of the waves, it was a minor miracle she wasn't. In one motion, Ray threw both paddles to Jim and he rolled his canoe right-side up. He pulled it knee-deep into the water as Jim hopped into the front. Before Ray could pick up the paddle that had been tossed back into the canoe, Jim was stroking at the water. With the constant wind at his back, Ray was confident they could get to Angie in good time - providing he and Jim didn't capsize along the way.

A well-defined plan of action bristled through Ray's head and with each rapid-fire thought, he yelled instructions to the man in front. Ray kept his eyes glued on Angie as he shouted. Jim nodded sharply with every phrase.

"We're better off in the heavier canoe…Grab onto the side and pull us tight when we get close enough…Jump in when you can, but don't sit on the seat…Get behind it, on your knees, we don't want too much weight in the front…I'll hop in after you, in front of Angie…It's got to happen fast, Jim."

Jim gave a final, decisive nod. There was nothing left to say. As they bucked and fought for control on the lake's surface, neither man gave any thought to the danger they had so willingly put themselves into. They were of one mind; to reach Angie before the lake did.

Ray had intentionally left out one key item he did not want Jim to hear. Not yet anyway. He was certain that Angie had taken on lake water. His own chances of being able to join them in the old canoe depended entirely upon how much of that water had collected into the bottom of the old craft. So far, the wood canoe had done its job exceptionally well by defying the wind and rolling with the lake's heavy swells. But Ray knew too much overall weight would create a lower, knifing effect; making it very likely that one poorly-timed wave could wash over the front of the canoe and sink them. Then all three would be lost to the lake. Ray was not willing to let that happen. If forced, he'd go it alone, in his canoe.

What little rain there was came in horizontally, hitting Ray's back with stinging reminders to hurry. He knew, if the clipper's storm clouds carried more moisture, the bulk of it may drop soon. And even though they were closing in on Angie, the prospect of facing driving sheets of rain only added to his sense of urgency.

Angie thought it was the desperate wantings of delirious thinking when she first heard her name being carried on the wind. "Maybe that always happens at the end," she considered. And when she caught sight of the shiny, bouncy canoe on the water ahead of her, Angie initially wondered if her mind was continuing to play dirty tricks. She squeezed the blur of lake water out of her eyes and looked again. It was still there. The silvery canoe had been no delusion; it was a glimmer of hope. The voice had been her Dad's and he was coming for her. Angie let go with a burst of tears as the renewed likelihood of her survival gained a stronger foothold against her fears of dying.

"Oh, dear God," she thanked into the wind. "Hurry...please."

If it weren't for the green of her eyes, Ray would've had a difficult time recognizing Angie. Her face was dripping wet and drained of all color, except for the light tinge of blue to her lips. Her hair was plastered tightly to her head, darkened and streaming with lake water. She looked taut and rigid, and though her jaw appeared set, it belied the absolute terror he saw in every feature. Every living part of her trembled, whether from cold, or fright, or shock, it did not matter; Ray saw she was beyond exhaustion.

And yet she paddled.

"Sisu," Ray thought.

When the canoes banged together Jim pulled with one hand at the edge of the old canoe, holding his paddle in the other. He bounced up with the crest of a wave and was gone in a heartbeat. He landed perfectly, knees splashing down behind the front seat. It was as if he had practiced the move all of his life. Ray could have kissed him.

Ray readied himself to copy Jim's jump, timing his leap to go along with the rise of the next wave. That's when he saw the camera bag slosh along the wooden ribs inside the boat. There was too much water. His added weight would only make things worse. Instead of hurdling aboard, Ray spun in place, and then, on his spread-out knees, he centered himself in his canoe. He stared into Angie's eyes for a split second, feeling that he was somehow letting her down. She'd given every ounce of her energy toward keeping herself alive and afloat. How could he possibly expect her to go on any longer?

But she had no choice. And neither did he.

"Too much water!" Ray yelled to Jim, pointing the floor. "Go without me...Now!!"

Jim nodded his understanding and plunged his paddle deep into the water. Ray took one last look as Angie surged past. She seemed better, less afraid.

"You can make it!" Ray shouted his encouragement.

The very next wave lifted the front of Ray's lightweight canoe too high into air, and the wind pitched him sideways. The second wave swallowed him whole.

Now it was his turn.

Angie and Jim hit hard on the shoreline's rocks, about a hundred feet north of the dock. Maggie spun circles and barked wildly at their arrival. Confused by failing to find her owner, Maggie ran back to the dock and sniffed around, trusting her nose to find Ray. Jim hopped out and skid the canoe as far as he could up onto dry land. He went back to Angie and gently peeled the paddle from her hand. She was slumped over, shaking, and still on her knees, staring down at the floor. With all the water now gathered at the rear of the canoe, Jim could not see her lower legs. He closed his eyes and shook his head, knowing they had just dodged a very big bullet.

"If that ain't enough to give a man a little religion, I don't what will," Jim said quietly. He let Angie alone for a few moments before touching her back. "Come on, Rose. You better go inside and warm up."

"Where's Ray?" she asked, not looking up.

Jim unfocused from his daughter and scanned the lake. He went to a knee, beside Angie.

"I don't see him."

Ice-out on Lost Woman had occurred the last week of April, a little later than normal but nothing that unusual. The spring rains had been light, leaving only the sun and wind to gradually eat away at the three-foot-thick ice pack that had covered the lake in winter. And given that Lost Woman was spring-fed, nourished constantly by cold, clear water, the lake's temperature had risen in small increments during the three-plus weeks following the slightly belated April opening.

In short, Ray had been dumped into some very cold water.

Before the end of most June months, anyone brave enough to venture into Lost Woman for a refreshing dip on a hot day found themselves wanting out of the water after only a few invigorating minutes. Ellie had always watched closely for signs of overindulgence whenever her youngsters swam in the cool, summer lake. Like all kids, Kyla and Ray would raise a mild fuss on her orders to exit the water. All the same, they were also thankful when Ellie would wrap up their skinny, shaking bodies into a warm towel.

"I could use that towel about now," Ray thought as he came up for another lungful of air. He mistimed an oncoming wave and was force-fed a large dose of lake water. He sputtered and coughed, took in a deep breath at the top of the next wave, and then disappeared.

The underwater breast stroke and frog kick were working well, so Ray was making good progress. The first hundred yards were behind him by the time he saw Jim and Angie reach shore. But Ray knew the hard facts of the situation; the second half of his lake swim would be extremely difficult. He could already feel the cold water sapping his strength at a rapid rate. His underwater sprints were shortening in length and he was spending more time above water, trying to replenish the growing need for more oxygen. On his next dive, Ray started counting his strokes as a way of distracting himself, so he could stay down a little longer.

"Five more," Ray thought, craving the fresh air above. "Then I'll go up."

He made it to seven...because everything started seeming so peaceful.

Maggie saw Ray first, at the top of a wave. Her shrill yelp alerted Angie to Ray's whereabouts just before he disappeared underwater. Angie pointed to where she had seen him, about seventy-five yards out.

"There!"

When Ray reappeared, Jim spotted him. Over and over they shouted his name, knowing all the while, he probably couldn't hear them. This was good though, he was getting closer.

"The storm's winding down," Jim said hopefully. He put his arm around Angie. "But say a prayer for him anyway."

Angie had never heard her Dad say anything remotely like that in her life. She reached for his hand.

"I already have."

Ray surfaced again and rolled over, treading water as he lay on his back, letting the swells lift and massage his stiffening body. The water didn't feel so cold anymore, diminishing his earlier sense of urgency. Besides, it felt really good to take a break. To breathe, whenever he wanted.

"A loon would never have this much trouble," he thought.

In the trough of each wave, Ray would lift his head to clear the water from his face so he could see the sky directly above. The fast-moving clouds seemed lighter to him, less threatening, and the lake wasn't nearly as rough. And it was a lot quieter up top, not so noisy anymore.

"Maybe, I'll still have time to get out on the lake before I go to work," he thought.

"Oh damn, my canoe…Loons are lucky, they don't need canoes."

Ray pulled up, vertical in the rolling water again.

"I'm losing my marbles."

He grabbed in some air and went under, restarting his underwater stroke. Time was running out.

Anyone who lived in Minnesota for any length of time found it impossible to avoid the subject of hypothermia. During a significant part of the year, coping with cold conditions was a regular part of life; literally in your face. From slight shivering, to frostbite, to coldwater drowning, most everyone, school age to old age, knew the danger levels and warning signs of overexposure. As Ray fought his way back to Pike Point he was profoundly aware, for the time being at least, that he was nearing an unstable stage - disorientation. Or, losing his marbles.

Jim returned quickly from the cabin, slipping and splashing along the uneven shore, a pair of blankets clutched under his arm. He draped one over Angie's shoulders and she pulled it tightly around her. She trembled in place as she watched the lake for signs of Ray. Each time he would pop into view Angie found herself releasing some of her own pent-up breathing. Although Ray was much closer now, she was growing increasingly uneasy. She was seeing him more often and it was obvious his forward progress had slowed way down, even though the waves were a third their former size. Then Jim said something that had been playing on her mind.

"Before he runs out of gas, I'm going to go get him."

"I know."

Ray had to change tactics. His underwater strategy wasn't working anymore. He couldn't hold his breath for any longer than a few seconds and his muscles were responding poorly to the commands his brain was sending. He was wasting precious energy trying to rise above and then dive below the surface. After a lengthy breather, Ray decided to set his bearings on what he figured was his dock. He started a weak crawl stroke, hoping his better judgment hadn't taken a temporary leave of absence. Trusting that his head still had a few good marbles rolling around.

For a while the new stroke worked to Ray's advantage and he covered half the distance to his goal. But the timing of his breaths and arm pulls began to fail and he was soon forced to swim with his face craned upward, to meet his constant need for air. It was a clumsy, inefficient stroke - and the only one left in his arsenal.

In short order the cold water drained the last of Ray's reserves and his cognition took a steep drop. He slipped into reflex mode and the steady rhythm of his arms lulled Ray's mind into a false sense of forward movement. He deteriorated into an ineffective struggle that barely managed to keep his head above the surface. In the end, with his muscle control nearly gone, he was only able to flail at the water.

When Jim tugged at his arm in the chest-deep water, Ray first thought he was being towed further into the lake by some sort of strange current. He fought to get away from Jim's tight hold until Maggie yelped him into semi-awareness. From a hollow distance, he heard a man's voice.

"Stand up."

The order made little sense.

"Stand up?" Ray wondered. "How could you stand on a lake? Except maybe in the winter…If it's winter, then why all the water? And who the hell is grabbing at my other arm?"

It was the woman's voice that made the most sense because she was telling him to do something he had been wanting to do for a long time.

"Stop swimming, Ray."

He obeyed her and was shocked to find himself suspended in the water. He thought for sure he would sink to the bottom.

"You can stand up now," she said.

Ray obeyed her once more and realized that she was right, again. He could stand up. And with their help, he could walk. Slowly, and with difficulty, he got to his dock. He steadied himself on a post and stopped for a rest, waist deep in the lake. He stared down at the plunking bubbles on the water's surface and became aware of heavy rain falling. The downpour felt warm, kind of like taking a shower. Someone trotting along the dock laid a blanket on his shoulders.

"Probably Jim," Ray assumed, turning his head slightly. He spoke to the incessant noise in his ear. "Quiet, Maggie."

Ray's swiftly returning responsiveness to outside stimuli was a very good sign. As Angie stood with him in the water, she quickly checked his pupils, pulse and respiration. They were okay, too. Even the uncontrollable, total-body shivering was a somewhat positive response. If not present, it would mean his core temperature was low enough to be worrisome. The weakness and loss of coordination, they were to be expected. Still, it was better to be careful.

"What's my name?" Angie asked loudly, concentrating on his eyes.

Ray looked at her and smirked the cutest, shakiest grin she had ever seen in her life.

"Enkeli," he chattered.

# 14

Jim opened the bathroom door for the tenth time, just after Ray shut off the shower.

"How you doing, Ray?"

"I'm good."

"Lois wants to know, coffee or cocoa?"

"Cocoa."

"Good. Angie said that would be better." Jim then asked, "Got any marshmallows?"

"No."

A large part of Ray wished they would all leave. It wasn't that he didn't appreciate their attentiveness; he simply didn't know how to react toward them. He didn't want to go through a detailed rehash of all that had happened, and he sure didn't want to hear an embarrassing thank you, from anyone. Nothing needed to be said because everybody was okay.

When Ray heard a car start up, he pulled aside the blind on the bathroom window and watched Lois and Jim drive away. He picked up the change of clothes Jim had placed inside the bathroom and got dressed. Angie was waiting for him at the dining room table.

"Sorry I took so long." Ray sat down, opposite the table from her. "Your Mom and Dad, they left before…"

"I asked them to go home," Angie interrupted. "I told them you probably didn't want a lot of fussing or talking right now. I know I don't."

"Thanks. I hope they won't mind."

"Mom understands. She always does. She'll explain it to Dad later."

Ray took a long sip from his mug of cocoa and felt the warming effects right away. Angie was right; this was the perfect tonic for him. He was glad to see that she had recovered nicely.

She had changed into the dry clothing Lois had hastily brought from home; a plaid-flannel shirt of Jim's and pair of Lois' jeans, both items being a few sizes too big. She was without make up and her hair was mussed and extra wavy from getting wet. Her arms were self-consciously folded in front of her, trying to hide the fact that she wore no bra. To Ray though, she looked gorgeous. When he saw Angie's big, expressive eyes were poised on the verge of an apology, he tried to stop her.

"You have freckles," he said, innocently enough.

His straightforward charm cracked Angie's fragile layer of composure. She broke down into an equal mixture of tears, laughter, and crying. She covered her face with both hands, ashamed that her emotions were so near the surface. Perplexed, Ray went to her and offered his napkin. When she saw the double ring of cocoa stains, Angie laughed more tears. She stood up and squeezed a bear hug around his neck. The feminine softness of Angie's body pressing up against his nearly halted Ray's breathing. She fit perfectly into his arms.

"I'm so sorry," she sobbed quietly. "All I wanted was a picture of you and my Dad."

"Please don't say any more," Ray asked of her. "Everything went our way."

The trip back to St. Paul was an overly long one for Angie. She tried listening to her music but soon shut off the disc player. For some reason, all the songs felt like unnecessary noise. When she checked her wristwatch for the time, she saw that the dial was fogged up and the hands had stopped moving at eight-fifteen. Angie smiled because the dashboard clock read twelve-eighteen. Her assistant Kate would be proud that she had fallen out of her constant, time-keeping habit. She slipped the watch off her wrist and tossed it on the seat next to her.

After an hour's worth of driving, Angie's legs, and especially her arms, began to stiffen up. Soon, her whole body started to ache. Sitting in one position became unbearable. Before she was halfway home Angie had to pull into a Seven-Eleven to buy a can of pop and a bottle of extra-strength Tylenol. She used the opportunity to fill up her gas tank and then drove through the local Burger King for a Big Whopper. She was famished.

Angie forced herself to drive non-stop the rest of the way home and three-plus hours later, she was happily relieved to pull into her driveway. It felt really good to finally stretch out, even though it hurt - Tylenol could only do so much. She made the obligatory phone call to her parents and informed them of her safe trip. Afterward, she stretched out on the couch.

Tina and Jessie arrived home with a flourish and woke Angie from her nap. Feeling much better after the brief rest, Angie traded hugs and small talk, and then went to her car to retrieve the souvenirs she had bought in Ely. Each girl received a duplicate of the small duck family that graced the top of Lois' curio. Both girls promptly named their mother ducks after Angie. They all giggled at the accuracy of the joke.

When Angie handed out their pink and white Lost Woman tee-shirts, the girls couldn't pass up the chance to poke fun at the possible double-meaning. Angie laughed with them, thinking she should have also gotten one for herself. The logo seemed to fit her frame of mind.

She ordered two pizzas to be delivered because it was fast and because she was still very hungry. Tomorrow, Angie promised herself, she would go back to her regular diet of eating healthier foods. All three ate supper as they studied together and by nine o'clock Tina and Jessie were satisfied they were well prepared for final exams. Angie excused herself to take a quick shower, planning to watch television in her room until falling asleep.

A little after one o'clock Angie sat up in bed, disgusted that her strategy for a good night's sleep had not panned out. She took two more pain-relief tablets and then tiptoed outside to her back-yard deck. She eased herself into a lounge chair, in search of a cool, soothing place to sit. The heavy night air and steady traffic noise from the nearby interstate did nothing to comfort her from the day's turmoil.

No rational person could go through the life-threatening chaos of Angie's morning without feeling at least some of the repercussions. Every time she twitched a muscle her aches were burning mementoes of the close call out on the lake. Angie had been confronted with something few people ever have the chance to directly experience; the sudden and certain ending of their life, coupled with the unexpected miracle of actually surviving.

By way of her tortured, last-minute thoughts, Angie had seen her short life ending with no opportunity for getting her proverbial house in order, or to say any goodbyes to all the people she knew and loved. She had imagined a pitiful, lonely conclusion to her existence, along with facing the stark reality that life held no possibility for a do-over. Her morning had been a personal train wreck in which she felt like the sole survivor. As her Dad had said; the experience was enough to give a person a little religion.

But Lois had always made sure that her daughter carried a portion of God's faith in her heart so Angie felt no need for a religious reawakening. What she did feel was the necessity to reset her priorities. The black storm that had threatened to destroy her had actually done Angie a favor by compelling her to reevaluate what was most important in her life.

The real truth, Angie realized, was that her first instincts had been correct. She had been fooling herself, or better yet, she had been blind to the fact that her nursing career had gradually become a top priority. The clinic, her patients, her professional time, had taken a front row seat when compared to her own personal life. As a matter of fact, her profession was her life. She hadn't even gone out on a date in over two years. Her social life was nowhere. And regretfully, her parents had been relegated to being only part-time slices of joy. Like it or not, what she had first stated to her parents was painfully true. Her life had little balance.

"And who came to mind when I knew I was going to die?" Angie questioned herself. "Not the clinic, or my patients, or even the girls. It was Mom and Dad…What more proof did I need?"

Angie groaned herself off the lounger and slid open the glass door of the dining room. She double-checked the lock, and in her mind, double-checked her agenda for tomorrow morning. Angie smiled her aching body down the dark hallway. Tomorrow, she would do the right thing, for her. She would go to the clinic and turn down the offer. She would rebalance her life.

Angie got into bed and crawled under the covers.

"Lois and Jim aren't going to be around forever," she whispered.

The nasty bout out on the lake had no lasting effects on Ray, other than to make him very hungry. After Angie left the cabin, he ate the lunch from his backpack as he toasted up four frozen waffles. He smothered each one in a disgraceful amount of maple syrup and chowed them down in record time. Jag would have been proud. Ray thought of him when he let Maggie lick the plate.

Although it wasn't nearly as warm, the bad weather had passed over so Ray carried a plastic bucket out to the old canoe. Before bailing out the water, Ray squatted down and ran his fingers along the white scratches on the outside of the hull. Jim would be disappointed. He picked up the floating return tag that had broken away from Angie's camera case and then emptied the boat of lake water. After he finished, Ray went back to the sunporch and set the tag on a window ledge, in hopes it would dry out in the warm porch air. Ray called for Maggie and then grabbed a short length of nylon rope from the Bronco.

Once the dog and rope were confined to the inside of the craft, he carefully lifted one end off the rocks as he set out onto the lake in search of his own canoe. He found it within five minutes, bobbing idly at the surface, air pockets and built-in bow floatations having kept it from sinking completely. He even located his missing paddle.

Having lived all of his life in the outdoors, Ray had no qualms about returning onto the lake. Many times, he had been caught out in open, heavy water; though not nearly as rough as today. And each scary incident had reinforced in him the total futility of fighting against nature's forces. A long time ago he had learned it was better to be humbled in safe refuge than to stubbornly die in a useless effort against dangerous odds.

Ray shuddered at the thought. Angie was lucky to be alive. Thank God for her strong will, and the hefty canoe. They had combined to overcome her rookie mistakes, in allowing for more time until help arrived.

As for himself, Ray had never doubted that he would live through the ordeal. Or more accurately, he hadn't given any thought to the possibility of not living. At the time, dying wasn't an option that merited consideration. Like Jim, his only concern had been for Angie. Both men had the deepest of feelings for her and, all others aside, they knew that Angie was someone special; someone well-worth saving.

Ray kept thinking of her as he towed his submerged canoe back to Pike Point. He thought of her frightened face, her strong spirit, and her tearful eyes. Even the funky clothes she had worn came to his mind. And when he remembered their bodies pressed together, with hers fitting so naturally up against his, Ray wondered how he could possibly wait until July to see her again.

"A month and a half," Ray said. "I don't think I can wait that long."

Maggie turned and woofed out her agreement.

# 15

ALL THE NEXT WEEK, ANGIE set about the task of rearranging life to her own liking. Once the job offer was turned down, she found herself settling in to a less formidable schedule. She cut back on her excessive hours at the clinic, re-joined a local health club, and spent any leftover time leisurely sprucing up the yard, replanting flower beds long neglected. She also made sure to call her parents every evening. Angie was relishing her extra hours of personal freedom in spite of being alone at the house and missing the girls. They had both gone home for summer break.

Along with Lois and Jim, Angie had made plans for their arrival on Saturday, tomorrow afternoon. Now that the house was empty, her parents would be staying with her. Over the phone, and well ahead of time, Jim had dictated a long list of materials needed for the basement project. He wanted to make sure there would be no delays, so the remodel could go ahead on schedule. And Angie, being somewhat like her Dad, had quickly ordered everything on the list, and had all of the items delivered as soon as possible. The whole lot sat in neat piles in her garage awaiting the planned start-up date of next Tuesday, the day after Memorial Day.

Angie was quite satisfied with all the changes she had made and her life was immediately better as a result. Her days were less stressful, less draining. More peaceful. She was somewhat surprised to discover that she very much enjoyed the time dedicated to her individual self. And quite frequently, Angie noticed, when her mind was unoccupied, little snippets of her vacation would come into view. The quiet beauty of Lost Woman, the look of contentment on her parents' faces, cute Grampa Maki, scholarly Roger, as well as many other short clips of her visit would make their brief appearances throughout her day.

Initially, Angie gave little thought to her pleasant flashbacks, attributing them to the aches and pains that were forever pulling her back to Pike Point. If given enough time to heal, Angie presumed, her thoughts of the past week would fade from the forefront. She was correct, in a way. Those physical cues did grow fainter and the scenes of her short vacation followed suit. Unexpectedly, though, the recurring images of Ray did not disappear. She would recall their first meeting at the resort, and the wild ride back from Skinny's. Quite often, Angie would see his red-faced reaction to her impulsive peck on the cheek. And when she lay awake in bed, Angie would remember the serious look on his face after their kiss in the boathouse. Most nights, she'd fall to sleep while picturing Ray's chattering smile at the dock.

During her second week home, when her girlish daydreams had reached a disconcerting level, Angie tried dismissing them away by telling herself they were most likely a delayed reaction to the dramatic lake rescue. Yet, at the same time, that line of reasoning made little sense because, after her first day at home, not one time had she re-lived the storm in her mind.

"If I filtered that out," Angie wondered to herself. "Then why does so much else stay?"

Angie's answer to her question came in the form of a large cardboard box delivered to her door, later that afternoon.

Ray's calendar was filled with the never ending cycle of work that was needed to keep the resort running on all cylinders. He stayed with his newly-formed habit of arriving on time and staying late. He also came to work clean shaven and neatly dressed; no more scrubby clothes and whisker stubble. It drove Kyla to the point of distraction. Ray said nothing, waiting patiently to be asked about his sudden change for the better while also making a private pledge to out-stubborn his sister. If that was even possible.

Their silent standoff lasted almost a week, until one day during lunch when Ray got his pay-off.

"What's with the new gig?" Jag asked a little too casually. "You slip on a rock and hit your head?"

"I don't know what you mean."

"Don't try to bullshit me, Maki. You're having a real good time driving Kyla nuts."

"Maybe…" Ray grinned. "Did she tell you to ask me about it?"

Jag looked around before answering.

"Yeah, she did. But you're not supposed to know."

"I want you to tell Kyla that she doesn't always need to know everything."

"I think not," Jag said emphatically. "I'll make something up before I tell her anything like that."

"Then stick with your rock theory," Ray said. "It's as good as any story you'll get from me."

Jag shook his head and sighed, "Pig-headed gene pool. My poor boys are doomed."

On the one week anniversary of the lake calamity Ray used his Wednesday morning to hang the old canoe above the fireplace in the lodge. With Jim's cleverly designed mounts, and Jag's muscle, the three men hoisted the canoe into place with no trouble. It rested high in the corner, suspended invisibly from the lodge-pole rafters, just as Ray had imagined. Ellie got teary-eyed when she first saw the canoe, recalling a private memory of herself and John. God love her tender heart.

Even Kyla approved.

"My eyes always go to the scratches," Jim said as he stood back to admire their work.

"Yeah. What's up with that?" Jag asked.

Ray gave his brother-in-law a dirty look.

"Ray won't let me paint over them," Jim explained. "Five minutes worth of work and it would look like new again."

They all turned to Ray, waiting for an explanation.

"I don't look at them as scratches," Ray told them. "They're more like souvenirs.

"Of what?" Jag challenged.

Ray only shrugged.

"There are certain times, Maki, when you are just too weird for words."

Though Ray kept busy, he still had enough time alone to let some self-doubts seep into his thinking. He wondered if Angie already had someone in her life. Or was she ever married? Divorced? With kids? No way, Lois would have shown pictures of any grandchildren. The fact that he knew so little about Angie started Ray to question that perhaps he had read too much into two simple kisses. How could he dare assume they had any sort of relationship from a slight peck on the cheek and a sudden kiss? Just because he was love-struck did not mean she was serious about him, or that she was even close. After all, he did have a history of jumping the gun. And in all honesty, wouldn't Angie have given him her phone number if she was in any way serious about him? She probably had a million other guys to choose from down in St. Paul. What she had said in the boathouse was probably the truth; she would most likely forget that they even had a date for the Fourth of July weekend.

Time, Ray felt, was running against him. He had to do something other than sit on his thumb and let his feet dangle. So, on his second Wednesday morning off, Ray drove into Ely, to St. Joseph's Church of the Holy Faith. He waited in the parking lot for Lois' catechism class to end. At nine o'clock on the button, a stream of happy kids blew open the church doors and skipped down the steps into a waiting school bus. Lois was not far behind. She spotted the Bronco and met Ray near her car.

"Last class of the year," Lois said, jerking a thumb toward the kids. "I don't know who's happier, them or me."

"Them," Ray answered.

"No doubt you're right." She asked with a grin, "Are you here for confession?"

"In a way, I suppose."

Lois opened the passenger door of her car, set her purse and some papers on the seat. She shut the door and leaned against the car, arms folded in front of her.

"Let me take a wild guess. This is about Angie."

"How would you know that?"

"I'd have to be as dense as Jim not to realize that you both have feelings for each other."

"Both?"

"Since the lake thing, Angie calls us every day. And she's not shy about asking me how you are. She also said that you asked her out on a date. She has plans for coming back in July."

"Well…good." Ray was suddenly out of things to say. "Thanks, Lois."

He turned for the Bronco. Lois tugged at his sleeve and stopped him.

"One more thing, Ray." She became serious. "I've always made it a point of not prying into Angie's business, personal or otherwise. But this time, things feel different…Anyway, I want you to keep something in mind."

"Sure."

"She's the only daughter I'll ever have."

"I understand, Lois."

One would almost think Lois' welcomed news would have a calming effect. In fact, the result was the complete opposite. For the rest of his day Ray thought of little else but seeing Angie again. As soon as he got home, he checked the return tag from her camera bag. Sure enough, she had filled in her St. Paul address. Then and there Ray finalized a decision that had been scratching at the back of his thoughts. He would drive to St. Paul and surprise her. Even if it was to just say hello. And if she wasn't too mad about the unannounced visit, maybe they could go out to her favorite restaurant.

The idea was completely rash and illogical, but at this point, he didn't care. There was no way he was going to wait another month to see Angie again. And maybe by showing up, Ray hoped she'd understand how strongly he felt about her. It was a fool's chance and he knew it, but one worth taking.

Ray started his plan in motion on Friday morning. After breakfast, he waited in the resort kitchen until only Ellie remained.

"I need to borrow your car, Ma."

"Sure, Ray. When will you need it?"

"Tomorrow, I'll be using it all day."

Kyla butted her way in from the dining room, hands full with breakfast dishes.

"All day tomorrow?!" Kyla said loudly, clattering the dishes on the counter. "You know darn well that's the first day of Memorial weekend."

"It doesn't matter whether you like it or not," Ray said frankly. "I'm going to St. Paul. To see Angie."

The two women stared at each other, speechless. And Kyla, being Kyla, recovered quickly.

"Well, that's altogether different. Take Sunday off, if you need to. We'll get by alright."

"Thanks," Ray laughed. "But Saturday is enough."

After signing for the certified mail, Angie carried the box to the coffee table in her living room. The original postmark, she noted, had been stamped in Ely. She hurried to the kitchen for a sharp knife and then slit open the tape, trying to guess at what could possibly be inside. Maybe it was something from Ray, she thought. More excited than ever, she pressed back the top flaps and sorted through the tightly wadded-up newspapers. Gingerly, with both hands, she pulled out the wood carving she had seen on Skinny's work table. She swept away the cardboard box with a slide of her foot and carefully set the bird down.

It was beautiful. And incredibly detailed. Holding the base that had been carved and painted to look like churning lake water, Angie rotated the loon in place. From every angle, it was flawless. The tall, white-striped necklace of the bird stood out brightly from the pearlescent, ebony-green head. The checkerboard back, the white underbelly, the glowing-red eyes and draping wings; everything about the loon felt lifelike. Plus, Skinny had scored innumerable fine lines into the carving to furnish the onlooking eye with the faux appearance of feathers.

"Oh, Roger," Angie quivered a whisper.

Ever so gently, Angie pulled out a small note that was bound to one wing by a thin rubber band. Sniffling a bit, she read the message.

*Angelica,*

*The not-so-common loon has adapted to living life in two distinct worlds; one being the secure, peaceful depths where the bird gathers sustenance and reigns supreme, encountering no ill. Even so, if our feathered friends wish to survive, they are forever bound to the callous, complex world above; a world not preferred, but one in which the loon is compelled to spend time, though always wary and ever vigilant. I, too, have lived life in two distinct worlds. It is in these respects that I liken myself to the species.*

*Yet, conversely, the bird in front of you also contrasts me. As you may discern by his posturing, he ably defends what he deems is his, a feat I failed to accomplish, long ago in my youth. This loon's story, unlike mine, will not be one of love lost.*

*In closing, please thank your parents for entrusting me with your address. Their thoughtfulness has allowed for my clumsy efforts of returning the sincere kindness you have shown to an appreciative old man. To paraphrase a very perceptive woman: I ask that you accept this gift, along with my written words, in the spirit in which they have been given…*

*Your newfound friend,*
*Roger*

*P.S. – I often thought of our good friend Ray while working on this carving.*

Angie sat down on the couch and re-read the note. As was intended, Skinny's admission of love lost tugged at all of the right heartstrings. And the thinly-veiled postscript reference to Ray's quandary was unmistakably clear. But it was the unwritten message that held the most meaning for Angie.

Against his strict principles, Roger was meddling into her private business. Yet, at the same time, she felt no anger or resentment. Angie knew that for someone like Roger to reveal anything confidential about his personal past must have been a very difficult chore. And he had sacrificed his rigid code of not interfering in anyone's life. He had done all this for her, because he cared. Angie was fully aware that the note she held in her hands had come at a high personal cost to the old hermit.

Feeling as though she had been gently pushed over the edge of something, Angie glanced at her new wristwatch and quickly cleared away the mess around the coffee table. She refolded the note and put it into her jean pocket for safekeeping. She knew the exact right way to respond.

Ray arrived home Friday evening to find Paavo sitting on the bench swing near the lake. Maggie scampered ahead to say her hello. The old man was an excellent ear-scratcher, and one of her favorite people.

"Hey, Grampa. What's up?"

"Ellie wants me to give you this."

Paavo handed over a folded brochure.

"A map of St. Paul," Ray chuckled.

"I never trust any map. Too many lines for me…But Ellie, she thinks it be a good idea. Your mother wants to make sure you get to the right place." Paavo rose up slowly from his seat. "You can walk me home? If I sit too long, I never stand up straight again."

Ray set the map on a seat and helped his grandfather off the swing floor. With very few words, they walked together in the growing light of a waning, near-full moon. When they neared the old house, Ray broke into the long silence.

"I'll be leaving pretty early. Can Maggie stay with you tonight?"

"Yes."

"Why so quiet?"

Paavo stopped in place. He made an effort to speak but his chin began to quiver and he was unable to give an answer. He turned away from his grandson, trying hard to conceal his moment of anguish. For the first time in Ray's life, the old Finn could not face him. Worried, Ray stepped alongside and laid a hand on his grandfather's trembling shoulder. Under his light grip, Grampa's bony frame felt shaky, and suddenly frail. The old man looked fearful. It was unsettling.

Ray gave him a little time to pull together.

"What's wrong, Grampa?"

"I have to fix something. And it be a hard thing for an old man to do."

"Is this about me going to see Angie?"

"Yes."

"I don't know what's going to happen, Grampa. Maybe nothing. You know me, I'm probably doing the wrong thing."

Paavo said nothing. He eventually lowered his head and talked quietly to the ground.

"Ever since you are born, Raymi…I always like to look at you. I can see in your eyes, part of me. I watch you grow into the best kind of man, strong on the inside and a puppy on the outside. Just like your Dad. And it makes me feel good to know that you will always be here, after I leave this place. But things be different now, because of Angie."

"What are you saying?"

"I say that Pike Point is my dream. I make a mistake when I try to make it your dream." Paavo pointed around with his walking stick, "This is a very nice place to live, and I always thanked God for that. But not one time did Pike Point hold me tight, or whisper into my ear. I give every inch of it away for a long life with my Augusta."

Paavo faced his grandson.

"You go see Angie tomorrow, and then do what is in your heart. I think that maybe, she is your dream. I think you can be happy with her, anywhere in this world."

Ray waited for his throat to unclench. He kissed his grandfather lightly on the temple.

"I love you, Grampa."

"You too, Raymi." Paavo started slowly away. "…you, too."

Ray actually stumbled when he walked around the corner and saw the Camry parked in his driveway. He stopped where he was and looked around, uncertain of what was happening, feeling like the ground had somehow shifted beneath him. He inched forward and laid a hand on the car, assuring himself that what he saw was indeed real. He double-checked the taillights. No mistake; it was Angie's car alright. Ray stared blankly at his cabin but all was dark. Then, from the lake side of the house, the back and forth squeaks of his bench swing jump-started a deep pulsing in his chest.

He approached without a sound, collecting himself as he did, allowing time for the sharp beating to subside. When he caught sight of Angie's silhouette swinging serenely against the backdrop of the moonlit lake, the deep throb restarted.

"Angie?"

She stood up at the sound of her name and Ray closed the gap between them. He brought the swing to a quiet standstill. They faced each other, nearly eye-to-eye, and close enough for him to catch a pleasing whiff of her soft-smelling perfume. With the most engaging of smiles, Angie tilted her head and handed over the brochure.

"Going on a trip?"

Ray blinked his eyes shut, bonding the moment to his memory. It was so good to hear the sound of her voice, to be enveloped in her presence again.

"I was hoping I could surprise a friend. And if she wasn't too mad, I was hoping she'd agree to have dinner with me."

"I would have liked that."

Ray looked down at her hands and slid the map from her fingers. He stared at the large lettering on the front, not sure of what to say. He folded the brochure into a small lump, making for a convenient way to fill in the quiet. Once done, he stuffed it into a back pocket. When Ray was able look at her again he could see that she had been regarding him closely. The pretty smile was still on her face.

"Why are you here, Angie?"

"Because I think you love me, Ray." Angie waited a couple of ticks, then pushed for an answer. "I'm right, aren't I?"

"Yes. You are. That day when you stopped for directions…You had me with the first look."

"That works out well. Because I love you."

Angie stepped off the swing floor and entered Ray's life. She placed her hands delicately on his face and with a light, electric touch, she kissed him. And he kissed her, returning the magic back to Angie. They looked at one another, each liking what they saw, each with the growing understanding that the person standing in front of them was exactly what had been missing from their lives.

Quickly then, they pulled each other close, kissing freely, pressing their bodies tightly together, eager to show the loving ache in their hearts.

And when the kiss was over, they held on even tighter, neither one wanting to let go, embraced by the greatest of life's gifts, the love for another.

"Oh, Ray," Angie whispered. "I didn't know that loving you would feel this good."

"It even hurts a little."

She smiled up at his honest charm.

"You say the cutest things." She kissed him again. "You're an easy man to love, Ray."

Angie laid her head on his chest and stared at shimmering glow on the lake. She slipped her hands under the tails of his shirt and wrapped him into her arms. She could feel the bare, beating warmth of his body, while sensing too, the inner strength of the man. It left her with another tingly set of goose bumps.

"Over there," Angie said, nodding toward the dock. "Standing with you in the water, when you called me that name…Enkeli. That's when it happened for me."

"I'll have to thank Grampa for teaching me some Finn."

"And I have to thank Roger." Angie snuggled closer. "Will you take me to see him tomorrow? I owe him a great big hug."

"I wouldn't miss that for the world." Ray grinned broadly when he imagined Skinny's reaction. "I can pick you up in the morning. Maybe we can have breakfast with Grampa before we go. I know he'd really like to see you. Everybody would."

There it was again, that innocent charm.

"We can do that if you really want to, Ray. But I was thinking about having peanut butter and jelly sandwiches for breakfast…just you and me. We could have lunch with Grampa."

"I like your idea a whole lot better. I'll even throw in some frozen waffles."

Ray then leaned back, out of their close embrace, holding her at arm's length.

"I have to be truthful with you, Angie. I've never felt this way about anyone. Nothing even comes close. And I feel like I'm in water that's over my head. I hope you know what you're doing because I sure don't."

Angie's eyes brimmed with tears. She reached up and clasped her hands behind Ray's neck, kissing him slowly, and gently, in a long, loving way. A tender, unforgettable kiss that sealed both hearts together… forever. Afterward, Angie looked deep into his eyes.

"I never thanked you for saving my life."

"We're even," Ray said. "You just saved mine."

# Thanksgiving Day
# 1997

RAY MAKI STOOD ON THE edge of his shore, looking out over the icy-gray water of Lost Woman Lake, ankle-deep in three inches of freshly fallen snow. In front of him lay a scene of peaceful, primeval beauty. The afternoon sun was indistinct in the sky and a soft blend of blue-gray clouds hovered overhead, their unmoving image mirrored on the surface of the lake. The snow-burdened pines of the far-off landscape and neighboring islands also reflected off the glassy water, in sharp contrast to the frosty, overcast colors. The wind was non-existent, holding back, unwilling to spoil the perfect picture.

All too soon, muffled shrieks of delight reached out to Ray and pulled him away from the quiet scenery. He turned toward the sunporch just in time to see J.P. being raised into the air, suspended upside down and dangling loosely, his foot clamped in Jag's tight grip. Thirteen-year-old Billy, in a desperate attempt to save his brother's happy life, hopped on to his father's big back and stuck to him like an argyle and corduroy-clad tick. A very pregnant Kyla, hands on hips, appeared suddenly and put an immediate, frowning halt to the noisy proceedings; a Norman

Rockwell painting brought forth into real life, and forever framed in Ray's memory.

An instant later, Jag casually flipped John Paul safely onto the short sofa in the sunporch. The big man crouched down and turned a bit, offering Billy's flushed cheek to his mother. Unable to resist, Kyla kissed her son and tousled his already messy hair. Quick as a blink, with her free hand, Kyla flicked a hard finger across husband's ear. Jag let lose with a short howl, followed closely by Billy and J.P.'s good-natured chortling. Then, giving the entire setting a second thought, Kyla planted a smiling, head-shaking kiss on Jag's cheek. She received several belly-pats as a reward.

Ray hoped for his sister's sake that she would have a girl baby this time. Whichever way, boy or girl, Ray was sure the chances were very high that Kyla would have her hands full, for years to come.

Ellie bypassed the wild bunch and partially swung open the porch door. She leaned out and poked her head past the edge, looking for Ray.

"I'm hungry, Ma!" he called out.

Ellie set her deep dimples into place with a quick grin and shooed at her son with a wave of the hand.

"Ten more minutes, Ray."

The unmistakable sound of snow being crunched under rolling tires prompted Ray to look toward the narrow road. He watched a car edge past his filled-up driveway and come to a stop. Seconds later, from around the corner, Lois and Jim walked into view. Ray waved.

And then, two miniature, three-year-old versions of Angie burst past their mother and ran out the door; green-eyed redheads that were full of life. Wearing emerald dresses and white tights, Annie and Amber scurried their patent-leather shoes through the fluffy snow toward Gramma and Grampa. A barking Maggie tagged along, wondering what sort of good food had been brought for her. Jim squatted low and scooped up the twin gigglers into his arms while Maggie sniffed at the air, very near to her new friend, Lois, who happened to be carrying a sweet-smelling crock pot.

"Tell me, girls," Jim said with a fast wink. "What's prettier than a red-headed girl with green eyes?"

"What, Grampa?" they asked coyly.

"*Two* red-headed girls! That's what!"

Jim carefully lowered his little angels onto the porch steps and followed them directly into the house, leaving Angie to prop open the door for her abandoned mother. Lois rolled her eyes toward Ray. He pointed to the pot she held in her hands.

"Jag's favorite baked beans?"

"He called to make a special request."

"Don't tell that to Kyla," he warned her. To himself, Ray thought, "I hope Lois left out the gunpowder this time."

In less than two hours time, anyone sitting close to Jag would find out.

Angie let the door close then changed her mind when she spotted Ray. Dressed in a thin, white turtleneck sweater, and black jeans, Angie folded her arms in front of herself to ward off the cold air as she shuffled short, cautious steps out to her husband. Ray watched her approach and unzipped his jacket when she neared, wrapping her into his warmth. Angie kissed his neck and pressed close. Neither one spoke, both relishing a rare moment alone.

"Finding any peace and quiet out here?" Angie eventually asked.

"A little," Ray answered.

She pulled her head off his chest and looked at him, trying to decipher the reason for his somber mood.

"I promised Roger and Bridget that I would bring them a turkey dinner the day after Thanksgiving. I'm sure Mom will watch the girls. That should be a quiet time for us."

"That would be nice." When Angie kept staring at him he asked, "What?"

"Do you ever miss it, Ray? I mean, the time you used to spend by yourself."

"Yeah, sometimes I do," he answered truthfully. "How about you? Do you ever miss the busy old days?"

"The clinic here keeps me busy enough. It's the people that I miss. Some of the patients, and the staff. I wonder how they're all getting along."

"Any regrets?"

"I have everything that I want, Ray. No regrets."

"Same here."

A rapid knocking on a window pane alerted Angie and Ray that dinner was almost ready. It was Jag's version of the two-minute warning. Angie squeezed tighter and snuggled deeper.

"I love you, Ray."

"I'm not surprised. I was once told that I'm an easy man to love."

"Your Mom said all of you Maki men were that way."

A smile appeared on Ray's face and a lump lodged in his throat. He leaned back, and with a light touch to her forehead, rearranged a small sprig of hair that had fallen out of place.

"I love you too, Angie." He kissed her softly. "More every day."

"Come on, Blue Eyes. We better go inside."

"I'll only be a minute longer."

Ray watched her scamper to the cabin. She climbed the first step of the sunporch and spun in place.

"Were you staring at my butt?"

"The whole way."

"Good. That's the way it should be."

Ray was proud of her. Angie was so good, so special. She was a loving wife and a deeply devoted mother. Whether at work in the Ely clinic or at home with the family, Angie was loads of fun to be around. Each morning when he awoke, Ray's first thoughts were of her. He was a lucky man and very thankful to have her in his life. In return, he made sure to give Angie the best of what was in him, because she always did the same.

And she had been a blessing to many others. Mr. Church got around better than ever. More than once, if someone dared comment on how well he walked, Ray had seen Mr. Church pull up the cuff of his pants to show off a shiny aluminum leg. He would tap the metal lightly with his beloved 82$^{nd}$ Airborne cane and proudly point out that he had an ankle joint now. "A damn handy thing to have," he would rumble. Last year, during the celebration their fiftieth wedding anniversary, Mr. and Mrs. Church had waltzed the closing dance at the local VFW; a simple feat they hadn't been able to carry out at their wedding. When their first-ever dance was over, there wasn't a dry eye in the house, including thirteen adoring grandchildren.

Skinny, too, had benefited from having Angie here on Pike Point. The mismatched pair had quickly become the best of friends. On a regular basis, short notes and sometimes long letters were exchanged between them, with Ray acting as the postman. Delivery of that private mail was a fun job because whoever the recipient happened to be, they always greeted Ray with a big smile. Whenever possible, Angie would volunteer to drive the old Bronco so she could haul supplies out to her good pal, Roger. Her visits were usually lengthy ones and, though Angie never divulged a word, Ray suspected that Skinny had opened up to her as he had never done with anyone else. Between Angie and Ellie looking out for him, Skinny enjoyed the best from different two worlds. He had it made. Bridget, too.

All was well and good, save for one thing.

Paavo was gone now. He had died quietly at home, two months short of his ninety-sixth birthday; after nearly seventy-three years on Pike Point. This was the second Thanksgiving without him and Ray missed him. Very much sometimes. But whenever that sadness came over him, Ray consoled himself by remembering that the old man had lived the best kind of life, in a place he had dearly loved. "The Good Lord's Earth," as Grampa used to say.

Ray would never forget him. And he would make sure to tell his little girls all about Grampa when they asked who the wrinkled-up old man in the picture was; the one in the center of the fireplace mantle; the old guy who was holding them when they were just babies. The great-grandfather they don't remember.

So it was up to Ray to tell them. He would be able to tell his girls of a strong-spirited, gentle man; an honorable, God-fearing man who you could always count on. Ray could tell the proud story of a hard-working, tireless immigrant who had died without having two of his own nickels to rub together, yet a man who had generously left behind the priceless gift of a never-ending love for his family.

You could ask no more from any man.

And, as soon as Annie and Amber were able to understand fully, Ray would explain that the words, 'P. Maki Guiding' were not just random letters printed on the back of an old canoe.

Those words had been his Grampa's way of life. Paavo Maki's enduring legacy.

The legacy of Pike Point.

Ray tried hard, but he could not stop the tears that rolled down his face. He raised his head and directed his eyes beyond the high branches above.

"Thank You," he said...over and over.

# Acknowledgements

SOMEHOW, UNLIKELY AS IT MAY seem, arbitrary portions of my life coalesced into the form of a book. Those who are partially responsible, I have listed below:

My great-grandfather, who, in 1922, became the first William Suhonen to set foot on Pike Point, allowing for his son, William E., to carry on the original dream.

To Aunts Virginia Short and Jeannie Stewart - your kindheartedness has made it possible for your brother, my father, to continue feeling his beloved Pike Point beneath his feet. Seventy-six years and counting. Your Billy lives his dream. Words fail. Thank you.

My parents, William and Mary Ellen Suhonen - two very special people who, at all times, blessed their children with the greatest of gifts - an unmatched, unconditional love. We, your six children, do our best to pay it forward.

My sister, Sandra Walters - your thoughtful encouragement, along with your medical expertise, helped make this book a reality.

My uncle, Vernon Galatz, World War Two veteran and proud member of the 82$^{nd}$ Airborne Division - from an early age, with calm courage and great character, you faced and overcame every challenge. We, all members of the Galatz family, could ask no more from any man. Your brother, William Galatz, Korean War veteran, stands shoulder to shoulder with you.

My maternal grandparents, Louis and Marie Galatz - numerous years have passed, and still, I often think of you both. You live on, in so many hearts.

The diverse cast of uncommon misfits whom I had the privilege to work with for more than thirty years - Take no offense. I fit right in with you misguided malcontents.

Jim Halberg and late wife, Lois - I pray that I meet with your approval.

Finally, and most importantly, the one and only love of my life, my wife Joan - you have given me your love, and the miraculous blessing of a wonderfully gifted, amazingly beautiful daughter. Our Vianna Rose. I love my two girls, more every day.